D0456948

Charlotte

CHARLOTTE

D. M. THOMAS

Duck Editions

First published in 2000 by
Duckworth Literary Entertainments, Ltd.
61 Frith Street, London W1V 5TA
Tel: 020 7434 4242
Fax: 020 7434 4420
email:DuckEd@duckworth-publishers.co.uk
www.ducknet.co.uk

A CIP catalogue record for this book is available
from the British Library

ISBN 0 7156 3004 0

Typeset by Ray Davies
Printed and bound in Great Britain by
Redwood Books Ltd, Trowbridge

I wish to thank Victoria Field for her important contribution,
both creative and critical, to the scenes on Martinique

DMT
Truro, England, 1999

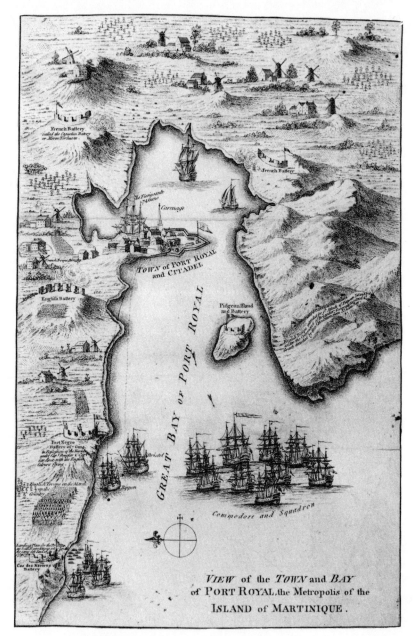

Martinique, French West Indies 1847

1

READER, I MARRIED HIM. A quiet wedding we had: he and I, the parson and clerk, were alone present. I have to confess that, viewless to my eye but vivid in my imagination, there was another presence. As the parson falteringly pronounced the dread words, 'why ye may not lawfully be joined together in matrimony,' my mind flashed to Thornfield Hall and the poor, savage creature in the third-storey room. Almost at the same moment I knew, with relief, that she was dead. Instantly I felt guilt at my sinfulness; and it was not assuaged by the knowledge that she had brought her death on herself, and was surely such an unhappy creature that death was merciful.

These feelings were swept away as we emerged from the dim church into a morning made all the brighter by the shower that had evidently fallen during our wedding, giving a sparkle to every green leaf and an added freshness and sweetness to the balmy air.

'So now you are Mrs Rochester!' said my dear Edward, drawing me into his arms and kissing me. 'You cannot escape me now, eh, Jane?'

'I shall never wish to, sir. But you – you may live to regret it!'

'Never, my Jane.' He pressed his mouth again to my smiling lips. 'Now let us hurry back to Ferndean. I care not for that sudden cold cloud;' – lifting his blind, leonine head – 'by the smell of the air I think it means to drench us. And though many waters cannot quench love, they can bring on chills – especially to someone as delicate as my darling wife!'

'Delicate, indeed!'

When we got back from church, I went into the kitchen of the manor-house, where Mary was cooking the dinner, and John cleaning the knives, and I said:

'Mary, I have been married to Mr Rochester this morning.' The housekeeper and her husband were both of that decent phlegmatic order of people, to whom one may at any time safely communicate a remarkable piece of news without incurring the danger of having one's ears pierced by some shrill ejaculation, and subsequently stunned by a torrent of wordy wonderment. Mary did look up, and she did stare at me: the ladle with which she was basting a pair of chickens roasting at the fire, did for some three minutes hang suspended in air, and for the same space of time John's knives also had rest from the polishing process: but Mary, bending again over the roast, said only:

'Have you, miss? Well, for sure!'

A short time after she pursued: 'I seed you go out with the master, but I didn't know you were gone to church to be wed,' and she basted away. John, when I turned to him, was grinning from ear to ear.

'I told Mary how it would be,' he said; 'I knew what Mr Edward' (John was an old servant, and had known his master when he was the cadet of the house; therefore, he often gave him his Christian name) 'I knew what Mr Edward would do; and I was certain he would not wait long neither: and he's done right, for aught I know. I wish you joy, miss!' and politely pulled his forelock.

'Thank you, John. Mr Rochester told me to give you and Mary this.' I put into his hand a five-pound note. Without waiting to hear more, I left the kitchen. In passing the door of that sanctum some time after, I caught the words, spoken in John's gruff voice:

'She ben't one o' th' handsomest, but she's varry good-natured and she'll do right by him, I reckon.'

And Mary's reply, softer, in a kind of muffled whisper, that sounded like:

'Well, 'tis better for'n than Graves' Pool.'

Moving away, I did not hear his response. My heart fluttered. I knew the pool; I knew that always murky, never sunlit, pool just beyond the northernmost boundary of Ferndean. Edward had had me lead him there, a few days after my arrival at the wood-shrouded manor-house. The sight of the water's still, black surface had immediately filled me with dread, and I was not surprised when, laying his hand on my shoulder, he said, 'I have brought you here to warn you, Jane. That pool, seemingly so shallow, is actually deeper than a man's height. More than one person has wandered into it unawares in the dark, and drowned. It almost seems to draw people into it. Don't walk near it except in daylight.'

Mary's muffled words could only, I believed, mean that she knew her master had – in his despair following the fire at Thornfield Hall, his blinding, and the loss of an arm – found his way to the pool; perhaps even walked into it, careless of his life; more probably, consciously wishing to end it. Mere chance, it was likely, had saved him: the nearby presence of John, or some other person, come there to chop wood, or pick berries. I shuddered at the thought of how close I had been to losing him. It was not something about which I could enquire, whether from John and Mary, or – even less – from Edward himself. I could only thank Providence that I had come back to him in time.

I hurried to my master – that is how I still, from long habit, thought of him – on his seat in the garden, drawing in the warm sun, which was again shining joyously after its brief eclipse outside the church. Bending over him from behind, I buried my lips in his unruly tangle of hair – for not even on this special day had he been able to tame it quite. 'How you have suffered, Edward!' I said. 'But you are safe now; and I hope I shall make you happy.'

My hand, resting on his shoulder, was quickly covered by his. 'Jane, Jane!' was all he said.

Mary and John, serving us dinner, paid their respects to their master, wishing him all happiness and thanking him for his generous gift. Then I read to him a while; but more absent-mindedly than usual, because my thoughts were still on Graves' Pool. It had been given the name of a seventeenth-century poet of this neighbourhood, Edward had explained during that first visit to the pool. 'He used to come here to find a melancholy inspiration, Jane: strange as that may seem.'

'It is indeed strange; I could find no inspiration from such a spot.'

'Yet the name is apt, is it not? For many a man, woman, child and beast has made this spot their grave.'

As I read to my new husband, I could picture the dread scene: Mr Rochester emerging from the trees into the pool, sinking almost at once to shoulder-height; another step and he is lost to life, and to me, and perhaps to God! Then, mercifully, –

'Master Edward! Sir!'

A groan from the desperate man. '– Is it you, John? Leave me! Leave this wreck of a man! Go home to your good wife! Cherish her!'

'– Jane! you read today with less attention than usual to the sense and feeling! May it be that you are distracted by something?'

'Distracted, sir?'

'Desist from addressing me as sir!'

'I like to call you sir!'

He ground his teeth. 'I think you are frightened of me, Jane.'

Putting down the book – as once a lover depicted by Dante had done – I approached him, put my arms around him, pressed his head to my bosom. 'Where love exists,' I murmured, 'there is no fear.'

'Good girl, Jane! Good girl!'

Silently I asked God to forgive me; for indeed there was a small amount of fear. How could it have been otherwise? It is not considered decent to express openly the fears which are bound to arise on a bride's wedding day; yet I possessed them in full measure. Reader, I was ignorant. I knew there were rites; knew that a marriage consisted of more than taking one's vows; I imagined – oh, how I imagined! I even longed, for what I scarcely knew! I knew my Shakespeare: 'The imaginary relish is so sweet,/That it enchants my sense!'

'Fear not, Jane,' he said, interrupting and soothing my thoughts; 'all will be well.'

'I am sure of that, dear Edward.'

I spoke truthfully. When the holy mysteries of the marriage chamber were at last unveiled to me, I did not doubt that he would be kind and patient. Yet I could not dismiss those apprehensions bred of my ignorance, and also my knowledge that he did not at all share my innocence. He had freely confessed to having enjoyed the favours of several mistresses – including the mother of Adèle – in his reckless disregard of all that is sacred, consequent upon his being tied to a mad, bestial creature. Those mistresses had lived in Paris, and other sophisticated continental cities; they were elegant and worldly beauties. I had become troubled, more than once, by allowing myself to drift into a fevered imagination of their seductive embraces, readily accepted by Edward. I feared, of course, that he would find me, by comparison, inept, as well as plain.

Mary entered, announcing a visitor, a Mr Bowles: an architect from Bradford whom my husband had invited to call, to discuss some business. 'I'll leave you to have your talk, my dear,' I said, kissing him on the brow; 'I have some letters to write.'

'Confound the man for choosing this day!' he growled. 'But it won't take long; then, I would like us to take a walk.'

Sitting at my bureau, I wrote to Diana and Mary at Moor House, to say what I had done: fully explaining also why I had thus acted. I felt sure they would approve my step unreservedly; and indeed, they would reply without delay expressing their surprise and pleasure, and saying they hoped soon to meet my husband. It was a harder task for me to write to St John, in Cambridge. I thought out what I should say very carefully. Having told him of the wedding, and my reasons, I concluded:

Dear St John, I believe God will richly bless your ministry. I feel sure that He Who blessed the marriage at Cana will provide for you a good and noble and pure wife, to help you in your labours. Marriage was not for us; as I have said to you before, I love you as a brother, and I hope and believe you love me as a sister. I do not love you as a bride ought to love her husband – as I love Mr Rochester – and nor do you love me in that way. You were right to insist that my coming to India with you, in an unmarried state, would not do; it would have given rise to too much ill-informed rumour and disapproval, and so hampered your ministry.

You may think me craven for not accepting the Lord's work in that far country; but consider at least that I am helping someone who has suffered blindness and the loss of an arm, in a fruitless attempt to save his demented wife; and this man has responsibility for many of the poor in this neighbourhood; therefore – though it is in no way a sacrifice on my part, because I love him dearly – I am perhaps serving a useful, if humble, purpose.

Affectionately yours,
Jane Rochester

It gave me an exquisite pleasure to sign both my letters with that unfamiliar name.

The gentleman whose surname I was now possessed of had very quickly sent Mr Bowles packing, I discovered. We could take our walk, hand in hand across fields, through lanes, over moorland. The day was now entirely grey overhead, yet unusually windless; the only sound, the occasional note of a bird, the dislodging of a stone by our footsteps in a lane, or the rustle of my dress-hem as we walked through wet long grass. Despite the absence of sun and colour, my heart was jocund.

We rested at last on a grassy seat, formed not by humans but by nature: before us, moorland and hills, receding endlessly. Seeming to gaze at the horizon, he said, 'Jane, do you know what I am seeing?'

'No, sir.' I could not, still, break myself from old habits.

'I am seeing Thornfield Hall, restored. I have given Mr Bowles the original plans and drawings, with some instructions for improvements.' The third storey, he continued, would be the most noticeable change; for he did not want either he or I to stare up at that window behind which Bertha and her keeper, Grace Poole, had lived – or rather existed – for so many years. 'Can you be happy there again, Jane, when it is whole again?'

'With you at my side, I can be happy anywhere. I was happy there before; I shall be thrice happy there with you at my side, Edward.'

'No painful ghosts, Jane?'

I squeezed his hand. 'No ghosts! And it will be good for Adèle to be at the place she knows as home.' Edward had found a school for her; I had visited her, and found her pale and unhappy, reminding me all too much of my gloomy school years; I was determined to have her home with us and to become her governess again.

'And also,' I added with a light laugh, 'I would not wish a child of ours – if Providence is kind to us – to grow up at Ferndean! It is too damp, bad for the health, and depressing in its darkness.'

'That is true,' he said. 'Our child – our children – shall deserve better than that.' We started our walk back, to that very same gloomy, damp, depressing Ferndean; which I confess did not seem at all gloomy at that moment. 'And you really and truly are not nervous, Jane? That is to say, about giving up your comfortable single bed, for one shared with this shattered, ancient wreck, your husband?'

'I am a little nervous,' I confessed; 'I know so little, you know so much; you have been with many beautiful women, and I am merely your plain Jane!'

'Plain? You think you are plain? Usually you describe yourself to me as positively ugly! Are you claiming that our rite earlier today has improved your appearance so much already?'

I stopped his laughter by drawing his head down and kissing him fully on his lips.

We arrived back at Ferndean, to a hearty tea. In the evening I read to him again, with as little concentration on my part. And so, our first day as a married couple was over.

And yet, not quite. Reader, you will expect me to draw a veil over the intimacies which transpire between a man and his wife. I am sorry to disappoint and offend you. I will tell you that everything seemed blissful to me; it was bliss to lie down side by side with Edward; to feel his passionate embrace and kisses; to feel my entire soul and being given up to him. The only surprise was the absence of anything that a married woman, except she were of the most puritanical disposition, could find displeasing or disturbing. There were a few moments of pain as I was deflowered – strange word, for something that seemed like a flowering of my womanhood. In the morning, when I woke beside my sleeping husband, I saw the small stain of blood on the sheet and I rejoiced in it. So pure was my love for this scarred giant of a man that I believed the blood to have come, tainted and sublunary though it was, from the same divine source as that which poured from our Saviour's wounds on the Cross.

2

A S I WOKE, I put out my hand to touch my dear husband, but found only the bedsheet, still warm from his body. I opened my eyes and saw, through a gap in the drapes, morning was already far advanced. There was a hint of bleak weather, not at all uncommon in our northern summer; but it did nothing to quench my buoyant spirits. Closing my eyes again, smiling to myself, I scolded myself for being a slug-abed! 'This will never do, Jane!' I whispered into the pillow. The delights of marriage must not blind me to my duty, which was to be up, dressed and downstairs betimes, so that I could help my husband in his breakfasting.

Excusing myself, however, that this was the first morning of my married life, for a few more luxurious moments I rested, eyes closed, my hand stroking the place where his body had but recently lain. I even fancied that I could smell his rough manliness.

When I eventually came downstairs, I found him seated at the table, eating porridge. His face lifted at the sound of my footsteps. 'Is it you, Jane!' he exclaimed. 'My darling wife!' The sight of his smiling face, framed by the greyness of the day filtering through the window behind him, made my heart flutter: just as it had done when I had first come to him again, summoned by his mysterious, anguished call for me.

Stepping to his side, I put my arm around his shoulder and kissed him on the brow. 'It is she!' I said, with a lilt in my voice – for there was so much happiness bubbling up inside of me. 'At last!

16

You must be thinking that, now I am safely your wife, I intend doing nothing at all save lie in bed late: but I assure you it is not so!'

'I know you better than that, dear Jane. But it would matter nothing to me if you did.' As the door opened and Mary appeared, bearing a tray with my steaming bowl of porridge on it, he added, 'You slept well, I trust?'

'Oh, very well! ... Thank you, Mary.'

''Tis a raw day, madam – more like winter. A day for hot porridge, that's a fact.'

When my Edward complimented her on the taste, she withdrew with a flush of pleasure on her plump, homely face.

I sat across the table from him, and began to dip my spoon in the porridge. I was not, I found – somewhat to my surprise – very hungry, and did not clear my bowl. I have heard that love, when it is acute as it was with me that morning, does have an injurious effect on the appetite. I prattled for a while but – finding that he was in a mood to be silent – contented myself with watching him. I noted with pleasure that he appeared to eat his food now with more assurance, more confidence, even than two or three weeks since; evidently he was becoming used to his affliction.

It is well known that in novels – for example, the novels of Miss Austen – the pen falters just at the point where, perhaps, the most interesting narrative begins: *after* the wedding ceremony. With the consequence that not only are the rituals of the marriage-chamber avoided but the ordinary, humdrum details of the start of a married life. To wit, how do you spend *the next morning*, or *the next afternoon*. Oh, I know that some brides are already ensconced in a carriage, being borne swiftly to London, or Scarborough at the very least; others are even being tossed on the billows – and no doubt thoroughly sick – on their way to even more glamorous destinations: Paris, perhaps, or Rome, or Venice. I will tell you

17

what we did. In the morning, while Mr Rochester discussed with the vicar and another local dignitary, plans for an improved water supply to the locality, I went on with sewing up some curtains for the back-parlour. And was thoroughly happy in my homely task! Together, husband and wife, we dined thereafter on the cold cuts from our braised chicken of the previous day, and Mary's delicious sago pudding. In the afternoon, as we always did unless the weather was atrocious, we walked.

Edward spoke, as we strolled arm-in-arm, of the encouragement he had received from his morning conversation. It was tragic, he observed, that so many people of the neighbourhood – having avoided the perils of the newly-born and of childhood – yielded to diseases in their thirties, or even twenties. It was due, in no small measure, to the inadequate water supply. He was determined, if at all possible, to do something about it; and I was heartily glad to offer to do anything a feeble woman could to help him in this worthy cause.

His sense of smell, sharpened by the loss of sight, had strength-ened; so that he was able to specify, with uncanny accuracy, every passing shrub, every passing bush. I spoke of the miraculous power of smell, which those of us who have normal sight so often allow to atrophy. I was thinking, I confess, of the tangy, altogether pleasant scent of his own body, which I had experienced so keenly upon waking. It may be that somehow he discerned my thoughts, for suddenly, after a period of silent walking, he said quietly:

'Jane, concerning last night …' He stopped; I waited, my heart fluttering inside my bodice. He did not speak. I was tongue-tied myself. I did not know if it was proper for a wife to express to her new husband such intimate feelings. I thought probably it was prudent not to. However, the silence became onerous. I decided to speak, but to give a light tone to my voice:

'I can only say, sir, that despite your incomparable ugliness I did not find your embraces at all unpleasant! Indeed, that was far from the case!'

He let out a sigh. 'That is good.'

I hoped he would speak further; but since, evidently, he was not going to, I added, in the same light, casual way:

'Of course, I am conscious of my inexperience, Edward. I only hope that you made allowance for that, and that I was not entirely displeasing to you either!'

He pressed my arm closer against him. 'Not displeasing, Jane; not at all.'

'Then I am heartily relieved.'

He stopped in his tracks, compelling me to lose my pace and stop too; he turned his sombre, handsome – and yet ugly – blind face to me. 'Jane,' he said, 'it will be better. Have no fear.'

He spoke in a kindly voice; yet I felt the anxious merriment die in my throat. I had to swallow hard, before saying, 'I'm sorry if in any way I was not to your liking.'

'You are entirely to my liking. Only, as you say, you are pure.'

We walked on. The unseasonably chill, grey day had seemed to cool and dim further in those few minutes of conversation. I heard him murmur that he believed we were passing such-and-such a clump of wildflowers, but I was in such distress that I do not remember what they were. Only that he was correct in his assumption, as I told him.

We did not refer to these intimate matters for the rest of our walk; and on my return to the house I hurried to help Mary in the kitchen. Edward had invited a few of the local worthies to a supper, knowing that they would wish to congratulate us – rumour of our marriage having flown around the whole neighbourhood – and to gaze upon his bride with curiosity. By such an invitation, Edward believed, we should spare ourselves many wasted hours as this or that gentleman, spinster or couple descended upon us uninvited.

I fear I did not listen attentively to Mary's prattle about the quality of the ingredients for the pie and the cake, being more and more overwhelmed by misery at my failings. I have observed that such histories as this conclude at the matrimonial altar: and it is because we writers are rightly fearful. In particular, every female writer, I believe, is a girl writing painstakingly, in a silent room, in a bleak, silent house, striving with a sense of desperation to be pleasing to her master.

The people who assembled that evening in our drawing-room were plain, decent folk, wholly unremarkable; it was all I could do to maintain a pleasant mien, as the hostess, because my mind kept reverting to his remark, 'Only, as you say, you are pure', and trying in vain to reassure myself it was intended as a compliment – though it had not sounded so: particularly following his earlier observation that 'it would get better'. It must be, I thought – as I strove to interest myself in someone's damson jam-making – that he compared me with his continental mistresses of a bygone era, and found me sadly wanting.

'Ouf! Thank God they are gone!' he exclaimed, after we had said our polite goodnights. 'Jane, pour me a brandy, will you? And then kneel before me and let me stroke your hair.' Hearing the glug from the decanter: 'Take a glass yourself, won't you?'

'No, thank you, it's too heavy on my stomach.' I put the glass in his hand and kneeled down at his feet as he had asked. I rested my head in his lap and thrilled to the touch of his hand on my hair. 'I wish I had luxuriant hair for you,' I murmured.

'Nonsense! It's like purest silk.'

The epithet allowed me to bring my preoccupations to the surface. 'But you are not so fond of purity,' I said.

In a tone of surprise: 'What makes you say that?'

Raising my head, putting my small hand in his, I first reminded him of his words, then burst out with everything that had made me miserable since our walk:

'I do not know whether the word "pure" is applicable to me. I suspect not. But I am only too well aware that I am wholly inexperienced, and I must appear clumsy to a man who has been married before and – when it proved unbearable – had many loves …'

'Not loves, Jane, not loves.'

'Lovers, then.' Getting to my feet, I began pacing in a small circle round the room in front of him. 'I am sorry if I disappointed you. You said I did not, but clearly you were being kind to me at that moment. You were more honest when you assured me it would get better; and that assurance, probably, was offered more in hope than expectation! You have made me feel a little foolish. Our' – I could not find the right word – 'union last night pleased me excessively; I believed at the time it pleased you too. Obviously I was mistaken. But I will try; I can learn …' I began to weep quietly.

'Jane! Jane!' He heaved his broad, wounded frame from his seat and moved towards me, stopping just to my left, holding his arm out to reach me. I moved quickly to stand directly before him; he stroked my cheek, brushing the tears away. 'You are speaking nonsense! I assure you, by all that is holy, I felt anxious that *you* had probably felt too little pleasure; had been disappointed in me. And that would have been very understandable, my darling Jane.'

'You are being honest?' Though I did not really have to ask the question, for his pleading face told me it was the truth. 'You do not find me too inexperienced? Too *pure*?'

'Too pure?' He repeated the word a second time: 'Too pure? Damnation, Jane, your purity is what drew me to you! It was, is, what I need, after a lifetime in which I have been too much in contact with its opposite, corruption, decadence.'

A weight lifted from my bosom and I breathed in deeply. Impulsively kissing him: 'I have been so silly!'

He smiled. 'Yes, you have been!'

I could not quite leave it yet. 'But you said it would get better; doesn't that imply some dissatisfaction, my love?'

'For *you*, Jane, I meant. For me it was beautiful, holding you in my arms so close, so perfectly close, kissing you ...'

'And I am telling you, sir, that it was equally beautiful for me!' Indeed, I added, no doubt the more so, since for me it was the first time; and any embarrassment or fear I might have felt had been swept away by the simple knowledge that we loved each other. His fears that he had in some way disappointed me were ridiculous, so – I pressed my hand against his mouth – we should have no more of this ridiculous conversation! My tears had by now changed to chuckles – from amusement at his foolishness; and he had been calling *me* silly! – but also at my own folly in wasting much of the day in a state of irrational misery.

Overcome by relief, I did take a tumbler of brandy and water after all, before retiring to bed with my loving husband. There, the chill of the room soon yielded to the cosy warmth of lying in his embrace. I felt, just as I had done on the previous night, a wonderment that any bride could find anything of shame, of defilement even, in the close marital embrace. Indeed, my dear husband slept when I still felt a craving for his kisses, his caresses, and I chastised myself for being too hungry for this joy which had suddenly fallen to my lot. I lay sleepless for so long, listening to his quiet breathing, the rattle of the panes in the wind, the hooting of an owl, that I felt an urge to get up again and go downstairs to read for a while; but I did not wish to risk disturbing him; I contented myself with tranquil and loving thoughts, and remembered scraps of poetry. In the end, I think I fell asleep in the middle of one of Mr Pope's tedious and artificial compositions: I have often found him a great aid to sleep.

I do not intend to offer an hourly, or even weekly, account of my marriage. Nothing could be more tedious. We lived quietly, writing, reading, walking, and discussing the renewal of Thornfield – and I was happy. My husband was often in a quiet mood, but unfailingly attentive and affectionate. The island of Jersey made an unforgettable impression on us both; he could not have picked out a sweeter spot for our honeymoon. Yet I was glad to return to the duller – indeed louring – environs where we had first met, to resume the ordinary habit of our life together. Fickle summer turned to an unusually golden autumn, and then the frosts came, suddenly.

Never did I weary of reading to Edward; never did I weary of conducting him where he wished to go: of doing for him what he wished to be done. And there was a pleasure in my services, most full, most exquisite, even though sad – because he claimed these services without painful shame or damping humiliation.

One morning, as I was writing a letter to his dictation, he came and bent over me, and said:

'Jane, have you a glittering ornament round your neck?'

I had a gold watch chain: I answered 'Yes.'

'And have you a pale blue dress on?'

I had. He informed me then, that for some time he had fancied the obscurity clouding one eye was becoming less dense, and that now he was sure of it.

Tears of joy sprang to my eyes, and I embraced him. 'Oh, dear Edward, that is wonderful!'

I asked him how long he had kept this news to himself, and he replied, 'A few weeks.'

'A few weeks! And yet you have seemed rather silent – even, at times, I thought gloomy!'

'I could not be sure. I prepared myself for a great disappointment. I did not wish to awaken in you hopes which I might have to dash.'

'Oh, you are so thoughtful! I so often misunderstand you!'

'I should like you to write a letter to Harley Street in London, to a Dr Arbuthnot. He did me the kindness of coming to see me after the accident; I recall his saying there was a possibility that in time a little sight might be restored to this eye; and if that were to happen I should consult him again immediately. At that time, Jane, such was my inner darkness, I gave no heed to his words – was in fact indifferent to them.'

'But now, let us thank God that He has been merciful.'

'Amen to that.'

3

SHALL I DESCRIBE all the circumstances of the first visit of my life to London? I think not; it has no relevance to the story I am telling, save for the encouraging news Edward received from a kindly specialist in Harley Street, whom we twice visited in the course of five days. All that I need tell you is contained, with much that is more pertinent, in a letter I wrote to my dear cousins some two months after our return home:

Ferndean Farm,
November 12, 1840

My dearest Diana and Mary,

I hope that you are both well, and still enjoying the experience of not being at the beck and call of some spoiled child, and even more spoiled mother. I was recently in the position of 'governess' myself once more – by my own choice – when we fetched Adèle back from the school where she has been so unhappy; but I have not been well (the reason for my not writing to you before), and my dear, caring husband decided it was unwise for me to undergo the stress entailed by teaching a girl who, for all her pleasant nature, is hardly likely to become a female Walter Scott or Humphry Davy. I did not relish the idea of seeking out a competent governess, and should never have agreed to relinquish my self-imposed labour had we not fortuitously heard of a very good school some twenty miles away; we took Adèle with us when we went to inspect it, and found it altogether lived up to its reputation for treating its pupils humanely. Adèle has, I am thankful to say, settled in happily.

There has been a wonderful change in Edward's circumstances since my last letter to you, dear cousins. He has regained a little sight in his left eye! He first thought he noticed the colour of the dress I was wearing; then could see the light of the sun. We immediately went to London for him to consult a very distinguished specialist, and that estimable gentleman prescribed drops and exercises which, gradually, have assisted nature in improving his sight, in that one eye, so that he is now able to walk without my aid, and even to read, with the assistance of a magnifying glass, for short periods. It is indeed a miracle, and we thank God daily for it.

I did not fail to make the most of my opportunity of being in London, as you may imagine. Our hotel nestled just under the great, awe-inspiring dome of St Paul's; every morning, awaking, I looked out and up at it, and was filled with a sense that it was the perfect earthly symbol of the supreme Deity. Nor, stepping into its solemn atmosphere, did I fail to say a prayer for the heroic endeavours and sacrifice of dear cousin St John, doing the Lord's work among heathens in those distant deserts. Have you heard from him since his arrival there? I suspect it is too soon. I could tell, from his short and formal letter after my wedding, that I had hurt him; but surely God will find a way of letting him know that a marriage, between people who do not love each other save in a brotherly-sisterly way, would not serve to further His cause.

I am heartily grateful that, as a consequence of St John's visit to Cambridge – and thanks also to you, who were able to give her my address – I am in contact again with that blessed angel of my childhood years, Miss Temple. Mrs Ashford, as I should call her. Her letters to me are as deep and spiritual as were her ministrations as the one luminous presence among the abominable adults of Lowood School. She is well-fitted to being the wife of a clergyman, and a mother (they have a three-year-old son).

I am hoping they will visit us next spring at the latest. Maria – how unused I am to addressing her by her Christian name! – has relatives in Bradford, so has promised to spend a few days here. And, dear cousins – dear Di and Mary – I would so love to welcome you here! If possible, soon – if you can tolerate our depressingly early winter (already it snows, just as if this were Alaska). It is high time you met my better half! In truth, there is one consequence of Edward's partially restored vision that – from a selfish point of view – I regret. *He* sees more of me – I speak in a literal sense – whereas *I* see less of him! He enjoys – and who can blame him? – the liberty of taking walks, engaging in business, etc., when he wishes to, without having to rely on my presence. The rebuilding of Thornfield Hall, which has commenced, engages much of his attention and time. I crave for those long hours of the recent past in which I read to him or wrote letters for him. There is still some of that activity left to me, but not so much. Understandably, he wishes to be as self-reliant as possible.

He is too caring of me; is anxious about my health – though I assure you I have nothing more serious than a prolonged bout of flu, lowering to the spirits but not dangerous; often refuses to allow me to accompany him out-of-doors, from pure concern that I not catch pneumonia. I tell him the harsh weather, to which I am well used, holds no terrors for me – and he responds that we were brought together again with such difficulty that he has no intention of risking the losing of me again. A noble sentiment, much to his credit as a husband; but I chafe at the restraint!

The diminution of my sense of purpose and service, as well as his too-great care, lead to my feeling often lonely. A visit from you would do wonders for me, I know; and so I warmly invite you – an invitation in which my darling Edward heartily concurs.

Yours in all affection,
Jane

This letter gave rise to a disagreeable conversation with my husband. Before sealing the letter I had been called away by Mary, our servant, over some minor drama in the kitchen, which she felt needed my personal attention. When I returned to the writing-desk I found Edward, still in his greatcoat, stooping closely over the pages, magnifying glass in hand. Hearing me, he lifted his back, and turned a stormy face upon me. 'Why – why? – have you written that I heartily concur in their coming here?' he ground out in a voice as cold as the flakes of snow dripping from his coat-tails.

Taken aback, stammering slightly, I replied: 'I wrote it as a matter of form. It's unlikely they will wish to come so far, in wintry conditions, and I did not think to trouble you when it would probably not be necessary to ask your consent. I'm sorry. It was a lie; a very small one, but I should not have written it.' Striving to understand my own action – because it was not my custom to be dishonest – I added: 'I wanted to reinforce the warmth of my invitation, while not troubling you unnecessarily.'

'Why would it have troubled me?'

'Not trouble ... I would have asked you on your return from your morning walk; but I was so sure you would say yes.'

His face softened. 'Well, I understand. If they agree to come, they are welcome, of course. It would be pleasant for you to have them here; and I myself would like to meet the two women who took you into their home. But Jane – I have to complain about something else, much more serious.' His tone of voice, and his expression, were what I can only describe as 'black'.

'What is that?' I said, alarmed further. 'Heavens, tell me!'

'You accuse me of neglect; of thinking more of my own liberty of movement – relatively speaking – than of your well-being; then, in another breath, of being some kind of tyrannical nurse, who keeps you shut up in the gloomy house! This is hardly just, Jane! You give your cousins too sanguine an impression of your health; I have been right to worry about you.'

'I am grateful, Edward – I did not mean to imply otherwise. Shall I tear the letter up?'

'And secondly,' he went on, without heeding my question, 'you often accompany me. Whenever the weather is mild enough, indeed. Twice this week we have walked together. You give a false, a deleterious, impression.'

'I will tear it up.'

'No, don't do that; I am perhaps unduly sensitive.' His face softening a little, he drew me to him, and kissed me. Drawing away, his voice quiet, affectionate: 'Surely it is understandable that I should take some pleasure in doing things for myself?'

'Of course, my darling.'

'I am yours, Jane: yours. Wherever I am, I see you.'

'I love you so much.'

And so the brief disagreement ended amicably. However, later I did rewrite the last page of my letter. I felt there had been some justice in his rebuke. The severity of its expression, however, left me feeling somewhat chilled, as if in reflection of the snow pelting the windows. Feeling unwell, I retired to lie down for an hour or two, giving myself over to unquiet thoughts.

Gradually these dissolved. Yes, it was true that he smiled, these days, less often than when he had been totally blind. But was it not natural that he should feel impatient and therefore moody? When he had had no hope of seeing again, he was forced to resign himself to darkness; but now, as his vision improved – but how slightly, how slowly! – he was impatient at once to be able to ride a horse, stride about at will, and so on. Yet we had been warned by Dr Arbuthnot that the vision would never improve to anything resembling normality.

By the time I had lain in bed an hour, my eyes closed against the dim, wintry room, I felt that I had had no right to be resentful in the slightest of my husband's chastisement. I had deserved far, far more severe chastisement for having written such sentences. His frowning, angry countenance reminded me of those days when he had sometimes chided me as a governess, and warmth stole through me at the memory. He was so good and kind, amidst his troubles – so thoughtless of his own comfort, even to the extent of denying himself the rights of a husband when he had seen that I had problems in getting to sleep: problems made worse by the influenza. Often he had merely sat on the bed, gazed tenderly down at me, and wished me a good night – to sleep, himself, in a much less comfortable bed, and deprived of those close contacts which are the secret manna of a happily married couple.

As I was thus savouring his goodness, and wishing for his presence, as if à propos ... 'Are you asleep, Jane?'

Opening my eyes, I saw his kind, anxious face. 'No, just resting for a while, Edward. I shall get up now. You were right, my love, to rebuke me; in fact, you were too kind.' Taking my arms from under the blankets, I reached for his hands.

'No, I spoke too harshly.' He kissed my brow. 'I ought to have taken care to ensure that you did not interpret concern as indifference or neglect. And as for your cousins, who were such good Samaritans to you – you had every right to invite them in my name too; for I long to meet them and thank them for your preservation.'

'All the same, I ought not to have taken your invitation for granted.'

I discovered how delightful it can be when lovers outdo each other in apologies, after some slight disagreement.

Assisting me to rise from the bed, he said, 'The snow has stopped, Jane, and the sun is debating whether to pay us a brief visit! Are you feeling well enough to take a drive with me to Thornfield?'

'Yes, indeed! I feel so much better!'

'It won't tire you too much, my angel?'

I insisted that, on the contrary, it would invigorate me; and a half hour later, in rare sunshine making the fallen snow sparkle like a million diamonds, we were on our way in the phaeton to that so-familiar spot. We arrived as the afternoon was turning again towards murk. 'Describe the scene to me, Jane,' he murmured, straining his eyes to try to see the ruined hulk. 'I can hear a bustling noise – is it coming along, the work?'

'It is indeed, sir. There are busy workmen everywhere. The ground floor is all but raised.'

I left him for a few moments, to explore – for a reason that euphemism would not wish to be named – some overgrown shrubbery. I returned quietly and, sensing he was in a private world that I should not too hastily interrupt, halted close to him, but outside his dim vision. There were tears in those poor eyes. I felt overcome by pity and tenderness. Not hard to imagine those inward pictures: the flames leaping up from the great house, the screams of servants burning or choked by fumes; he, dashing in to try to rescue the mad wife who had wrought this havoc and who was standing on the battlements, her long black hair streaming against the flames; his climbing up through the skylight to reach her, only to hear her give one last mad yell and leap to her death … At last I took his arm, and he gave a start. 'Jane!'

'You are not to distress yourself, my love,' I said. 'You did all that any man could do to save them; and at what a frightful cost to yourself!'

I could sense him fighting with his emotions. When he spoke it was in almost a whisper: 'One and twenty years ago to the precise day, Jane, I was married to that wretched creature – married under a burning tropical heaven, amid brilliant, giant flowers and plants that gave a delusory hope of mutual happiness.'

'A sad anniversary, then; a day of grief indeed!'

'Well – yes. And I fear it was somewhat responsible for my ill humour this morning.'

'Since when did you have to have a special reason to be in an ill humour, sir?' I demanded playfully; and he gave a wintry smile, nodding. I continued: 'But I wish you had told me; you cannot help but be affected by the remembrance – called up by an anniversary – of such a dismal event.'

At that moment I saw Mr Bowles the architect, a gentleman almost as round as his name, puffing from the effort of hurrying through the snow towards us. We greeted him, and I walked away, leaving the two men to their business.

We travelled back through the dark. I arrived home cold and exhausted, yet content and refreshed. We welcomed Mary's warming mutton stew. As my husband made to kiss me goodnight, on the landing, I said to him, 'You are welcome – more than welcome, sir – to sleep in your own comfortable bed tonight! My chest is clear; I shall sleep easily.'

He hesitated. 'Are you quite sure?'

'Quite.'

'Then I accept with pleasure!'

Our union was delicious, though too brief. Very quickly, as if the emotional stresses of the day suddenly overcame him, he was asleep. Nor was I far behind him, my arm still loosely embracing his beloved form.

Just two or three days later I received a letter bearing the unmistakable handwriting of Diana. Surprised – delighted – that mine to them had been answered so speedily, I tore it open. As ought to have been obvious to me, my letter had not yet reached them. Diana expressed their anxiety over not having heard news of me; told me St John had arrived safely in Calcutta, after a stormy and unpleasant voyage, during which no fewer than four of the passengers had required his spiritual ministrations when they sickened and died. She and Mary missed him very much; and missed even the company they had once found in their slavery as governesses. They scarcely knew what to do with their time. They were considering the possibility of taking ship for India themselves, to join St John and try to be of service to him and his pagan flock.

Having hoped I would be reading a promise to visit, I felt somewhat downcast: not helped by the dreary aspect of the January day. What helped to jolt me out of my selfish, self-pitying mood was a different Mary – wiping her floury gnarled hands on her apron – rushing into the room and crying, 'Th'master wants you to come out and see!' I followed her. Outside, there was Edward, proudly mounted on his favourite horse. John was holding the reins, leading Bessie on a slow walk. Master and servant both had broad grins on their faces. Seeing me, Edward lifted his good arm in triumph. At a command, John gave the reins into his hand, and Edward goaded Bessie into a trot. The steed started at a sudden bird – reared up – my heart was in my mouth. Edward controlled her, dismounted, and hastened towards me.

'Well, it's a start, Jane!'

'I'm so pleased to see it! But you must take care!'

He laughed. 'I promise.'

Aglow from his pleasure, I went back in an altogether lighter frame of mind to peruse Diana's letter more carefully. I resolved to write again, urging caution before any such rash move. India would be perilous for their health, as it would have been for mine. I could understand their feeling an emptiness in their lives, now that they had just enough money to lead independent lives; but both were attractive enough in character and looks to find good husbands, if only they were patient. And if they did not, there was much that they could do to make their lives productive. They could read widely, practise their many talents, throw themselves into charitable causes. Not least, I felt, they could visit me.

When winter was showing the first faint signs of spring, I received a letter from St John himself. His missive shocked me, drained me of vitality – such vitality as I still had, after too many dark months – and left me much disturbed.

After some eloquent paragraphs concerning the difficult voyage, the heat, disease and desolation which he discovered upon arrival, and his ministration to some fifty infidel souls, he continued:

Dear sister, I wish to apologise for the churlish brevity of my letter following upon your marriage to Mr Rochester. It was unworthy of a Christian. I do indeed wish you happiness.

I also wish that I had opened up my heart to you. That cold heart, which you scorned so much! My heart was far from cold. Sometimes I wondered why you could be so blind to my feelings. I trembled with desire and longing in your presence. All other apparent amorous predilections – I am thinking of course especially of the charming but uninteresting Rosamond Oliver – were essentially masks to hide my real passion. Which was entirely for you, dear Jane. I write this while recognising the folly, and indeed indiscretion, of addressing a married woman in such a way. But now it matters not.

From the moment I saw you, I recognised a trait in you which made me your slave forever: a passionate quality, all the more powerful because I am sure you yourself were unconscious of it. Every movement of your body, your eyes, your lips, bespoke an ardent, impassioned nature. But your passion was turned elsewhere. Pride made me hide my own passion; and I am sufficiently schooled in hiding my own tendency towards wild thoughts – wanton thoughts – before my sisters, to have been able to behave with you in the same well-disciplined way. As if I were marble, as I once overheard you describing me!

Aware that love could not tempt you to wed me, but only your large sense of duty and responsibility, I 'played that card' (a phrase used by a rather ruffianly, dissolute companion on the ship), urging you to accompany me – yes, as my wife, but really to serve our Lord. It was, I now feel, a grave error. If only I had said, I want you as my wife – and I do not care whether you serve the Lord! Probably if I had declared my love, it would still not have persuaded you; but I would have been truthful, at least; and so I would not now be tormented, as I am, by vain regrets.

I hope I have something to give to God; yet I know my vices. It may be I shall marry, in the next few weeks, one of my parish, a young girl of fifteen, who is ignorant but teachable, to an extent. However, she is not you, Jane – not you. One kiss, innocently on the cheek, from you, seemed to contain all the poetry and passion of Shakespeare and Byron. I say it sorrowfully: for if you were not a secret child of passion, you would not so strongly have craved another, and I should doubtless have been able to bring you along with me.

It was not to be.

Yours ever,
St John

I did not think it necessary or advisable to show his letter to my husband. I was struck by the incongruity that Edward had complained of my being too pure; whereas St John lamented that I was too passionate: a truth about myself that I had never doubted.

My first impulse was that I should burn his letter; but then it seemed to me ungrateful to do so. He had expressed his feelings so painfully, courageously even, and the least I could do was to keep it; only making sure that I hid it well. It was, after all, not precisely a love-letter; more a letter renouncing love.

Writing this true history, dear reader, while a pulsing sun lights up the brilliant colours of trees, shrubs and flowers, just outside the patch of shade in which I sit – observing brown and black figures going about their labours – I can scarcely believe this is the same Jane who read that letter, barely two years ago, in a dour, damp house – and the only colour, outside, the few primroses struggling out of snow! I am happy, fulfilled; I suspect not for long, since a fortune-teller has predicted that if I found happiness I would not live long to enjoy it. Still, I am happy – yet my brain swirls from the sheer unreality of all the changes that have occurred in my life: both tragic and joyous. It is so with all lives. No novel, whether a virile, rumbustious concoction by Mr Fielding, an urbane social comedy by Miss Austen or – dare I say it? – a gloomy, muffled romance by one of the Miss Brontës, can be more than a feeble echo of what actually occurs to all of us. Even though we weep over tender death-bed scenes, do we not read and write novels in order to escape from the sheer terror of real life? Even sudden happiness is, in its way, terrible.

4

SUMMER DREW ON – the second summer of my marriage to Edward – and 'the even tenor of my ways' was interrupted most happily by a visitation from years long gone and unmourned.

'I have thought about you often, Jane, over the years; hoping that you would find happiness in your life.'

Maria Ashford – the former Miss Temple of my Lowood days – drank tea with me in the parlour; and neither of us either could, or wished to, suppress our smiles of delight.

'Well, as you see, I have found it – against the odds.'

She nodded. 'I feared for you. You had so much character and intelligence, but you were poor; and, while your appearance was pleasing, you were obviously not going to turn into a beauty, such as might make a man forget about your poverty. In that respect, I saw my younger self in you. For I, too, was no beauty, and poor.'

'Oh, but you *were* beautiful, Miss Te– Maria! You still are!'

'That's nonsense. I tried to teach you to tell the truth, Jane; you disappoint me.' Her fine dark brown eyes twinkled humorously. 'At thirty-five, I know I am even less pleasing to the eye than I was at Lowood. But no matter: we can say we are two ladies who have been lucky enough to find husbands sensible enough to look below the surface. I like your Edward; even from our short encounter' – Edward had greeted her on arrival just before a necessary journey to Thornfield – 'I am sure I am going to like him even better as I get to know him.'

I told her I was sorry not to have the opportunity to meet her husband; and I longed also to see her little son, Arthur, whom she had left with her sister-in-law, in Bradford, while she made this visit to me. Her eyes grew soft and distant, as she said what a beautiful child he was – all the more dear since she had had, both before and after his birth, suffered miscarriages. And her husband, William, she said, was admirable in all respects: she felt that she scarcely deserved him.

I recalled, and related to her, the distress of all her pupils at Lowood School, when we learned she was to leave us to get married: 'None of us believed there was a man in the whole world who was worthy of our Miss Temple! For truly you were *our* Miss Temple! No one else had any right to ownership of you, not even yourself!'

Maria laughed: like a bell, clear and bright and resonant. I had never seen her laugh at Lowood, though she had blessed us constantly with affectionate smiles. It was clear that she was happy in her new life. Her letters to me had implied as much – but a woman's features tell the truth much more plainly and certainly. 'Oh, I assure you,' she said, 'William is more than worthy of me. It is indeed a shame that he could not come with me this time. He has a merry, affable, engaging personality.'

It was thanks to his outgoing nature that she had had news of me this past winter; for none but an affable, outgoing man would have engaged such an austere figure as St John Rivers in conversation, at the church meeting in Cambridge which she had attended with her husband. 'How fortuitous it was, Jane, that Mr Rivers mentioned the name "Jane Eyre", when speaking of his plans for India! It was not necessary for him to speak your name, but I had the impression that he *wished* to utter a name that was occupying all his thoughts ... Or, if not quite all his thoughts, certainly jostling with God for his preoccupation! You were saying you received a letter from him: tell me ...'

Having perused it many times till I almost knew it *verbatim*, I revealed to her all the contents of St John's letter, save its heart, its essence. And yet this, too, I revealed to her the next day, by which time we knew we had become, no longer simply a favourite teacher and favourite pupil, but firm, trusting friends. I took joy in her company, and already grieved that she must leave tomorrow. Though late arriving home from Thornfield, and forced to leave us early to look over some documents demanding his urgent attention, Edward had behaved most warmly to her; they had enjoyed each other's company.

Maria and I shed tears over sad memories of Lowood: in particular, the death of my dear friend Helen, whom she had so lovingly attended in her illness. We also, to my surprise, laughed over incidents which had not seemed in the least amusing at the time; and she reminded me of a line from Ovid stating that even sad happenings might one day be recalled with happiness.

We shared confidences during a walk on the moor. She told me of her sadness that the last miscarriage would prevent her from having any more children; that William had been in low spirits as a consequence of that. I confessed my fears – having been married for almost a year – that I might let Edward down by being unable to conceive. She reassured me by saying it had been over a year before her first conception; I must be patient and it would happen. I drew strength from her words, as I had done so often at Lowood.

That evening, she and I again sat up late, before a roaring fire. I felt sad at the thought of her leaving so soon, and asked her to consider staying just one more day. I watched her struggling between desire to please me, and longing to see Arthur again. Finally she agreed to stay; she had forewarned her sister-in-law that it was possible she would remain another night, so they would not be worried.

We gazed companionably into the fire. I became sad for no reason; her kind, shrewd eyes remarked it. 'You are too much alone here,' she said; 'it will be good for you when you have your own little baby to care for, my dear.'

'Yes, that is true; I long for it with all my heart.'

Involuntarily, I sighed. Tall and upright in her chair, her dark eyes shining – reminding me of so many evenings at Lowood, for physically she had changed little, apart from having gained a little weight; while her mind, her spirituality, her wisdom, had altered not a whit – she murmured: 'Jane, I trust there is nothing wrong concerning the intimate side of things with Edward? Forgive me for asking such a question; but I am your friend; I think you have few friends – at least among married women. Bluntly, do you still share a bed?'

'Oh, yes!' I exclaimed, smiling. 'Not always – for I have often been sick, or finding difficulty in sleeping; but normally, yes, I assure you we share a precious closeness!'

'That is good. It is important. For the man, the husband. For us women its main importance, I feel, is to keep our husbands happy and at home.'

'I don't share that feeling. It's important to me too. To feel the physical warmth, the closeness of bodies as well as souls.'

'I am glad. All is well with you. Edward is a good deal more taciturn than my William, but most amiable.'

'You are right that I lack married friends to talk to, among people I could trust with confidences. I am still quite an ignorant girl – not so much more advanced than when you were my teacher! There is one thing … but it is quite intimate …'

'Have no fear. Recall, you saw Byron on my bookcase!'

'That is so!' I gathered my courage and at last said in a low voice:

'I have wondered how the husband's ... finger can convey the male seed into the womb.'

Her eyes widened. 'But it cannot.'

'Then – how is it transferred?'

She leaned forward, gazing down at me intently (I had arranged myself on the floor, my skirts around me). 'Through his member, of course.'

I was silent, running my hand several times across my small bosom.

'Jane, he does penetrate you, does he not?'

'Oh, yes,' I said, embarrassment and perturbed. 'With his finger. Is this not normal?'

She slid from her chair, down onto the floor next to me. 'Yes, sometimes, as a preliminary to intercourse.'

My thoughts and feelings were in tumult. 'Then, Maria, with us the preliminary is the intercourse itself.'

'Oh, my poor innocent Jane Eyre!'

'I have assumed that somehow, without my remarking it, he touched his member before entry with his finger. It's true that – I have felt – something was not quite complete. I am not so ignorant that I did not feel the male member should somehow be more involved ... but I have been confused ... It seems ... it seems ... too soft and small to enter.'

'It should grow hard, Jane – hard and long. Is that not so with Edward?'

I replied faintly, 'I have touched it two or three times, and it has always seemed soft. Soft and small.'

'He does not strike me as an unmanly man,' she reflected, her hand stroking my shoulder. 'I am sure it must be of a medical nature, which no doubt can easily be cured. You must talk to him frankly, and urge him to take medical advice.'

'We talked at the start of our marriage, a little, about the physical side; but I decided it was not wise, that it created misunderstandings.'

'Well … think about it. Silence between you has certainly not diminished misunderstanding … It's late; the long walk this afternoon has wearied me most pleasantly.'

'I must retire too.'

We kissed goodnight; when she had climbed the stairs, I tiptoed to my husband's study; the door was ajar; I saw he was still bent over papers, holding them close to his eyes; decided not to disturb him, but instead walked outside. It was a mild, clear night; soon a host of stars clustered in their familiar patterns in the sky. I walked, scarcely knowing in which direction. Shame and a sense of my worthlessness filled me. I was still a virgin! My husband found me disgusting, or at best neutral, without appeal. Nor could I blame him; I was small, plain, uninteresting. But why had he not discovered his distaste before our marriage? Evidently it was something about my person that only became apparent to him on close, intimate contact.

I felt ashamed, also, of my stupid ignorance. I had taught crude village girls, during my time with Mary and Diana. One could not help overhearing some of their private exchanges, often accompanied by coarse merriment. I knew – at some level of my mind – that the *penis* was involved in sexual intercourse, and underwent certain changes. I even recalled – though for ten years I had tried to forget it, and even succeeded – a disgusting moment in my childhood, when Mrs Reed's son John, stout and loutish, entered my bedroom in a state of undress, attempting (successfully) to shock and frighten me.

I knew! And yet I did not know! I even recalled – I thought – wondering if only beasts, including human ones like John Reed, used the male member; whereas more civilised beings had devised a more delicate form of procreation; and that perhaps Edward deliberately suppressed any physical reaction so as not to perturb me. As Maria had said, poor innocent Jane Eyre!

Each passing month I had hoped for the first signs of pregnancy; yet I was still a virgin … It was unbearable, to have been so stupid. Unbearable, above all, not to have been able to stir the least desire in my husband.

I had been walking blindly among thick trees, their foliage blotting out all the stars. Suddenly I had reached the end of them – was about to step forward on clear ground – and found, just in time, the slime-covered water of Graves' Pool. I poised on the very brink. A wild desire to walk straight into it came upon me: to put an end to a worthless life.

I think I was only restrained by concern for Maria. If I took my life, tonight, she would blame herself for the tragedy. I could not wish such pain on someone so kind, so good. I withdrew into the trees, and made my way back to the house.

I crept past my husband's study and, weeping, took off my clothes and went to bed. It was a long time before I attained the brief, happy oblivion of sleep; at which time Edward still had not come to bed. This tardiness of his had been evinced more and more often.

Reader, this is a very different picture of my marriage from that which you were presented with in what I would call my 'romantic' version. Reality, however, does not often coincide with romance. I will remind you: 'When his firstborn was put into his arms, he could see that the boy had inherited his own eyes, as they once were – large, brilliant, and black …' Well, events did not quite happen like that.

That night I had a dream in which I met my father for the first time – in a vicarage perched precariously on high cliffs. He and I looked out onto stormy billows. He had dark features, and ex-plained to me that he had not died in my infancy from typhus fever but had gone to India. He produced from his pocket a small curled-up snake. It was not dangerous, he said; and if I talked to it gently it would uncoil itself. It did so, and swayed its head in front of me. Even the billows calmed. The dream, comforting and disquieting in equal measure, lingered until it was overcome by the misery of my present situation.

At breakfast, Maria's eyes could not quite meet mine; just as mine avoided meeting Edward's. He did not seem to notice the uneasy atmosphere, but talked amiably enough to us. Soon he was up and gone, and Maria and I were left together. I felt that she regretted having promised to stay an extra day, and so I assured her I would understand if she wished to change her mind. No, she said, she would stay – and was happy to stay. I confess I felt relieved. This day I did not want to be left.

Edward being away at Thornfield – and then, in the evening, dining at a hotel with a banker, to arrange additional financial support for the re-building of Thornfield, which was proving to be expensive – I had all day with Maria to pour out the pain that was in my heart. I did not stint. I told her that our nuptial embraces – stopping short of intercourse – had grown more and more infrequent over the months. He was up betimes, and late to bed. When, rarely, we had been together, his kisses and caresses, I could now confess to myself, were half-hearted. Hitherto I had ascribed all this to the demands of his project, which consumed much of his time and energy.

Yet – I was weeping as I spoke – even when he was not at Thornfield, I saw little of him. He could now see well enough to ride without anyone accompanying him; not at a gallop, nor even safely at a trot; but he could ride with caution, and this was a great joy to him. It would have been churlish of me, I said, to have begrudged him that exercise. But as a consequence, living in this benighted spot, I was reduced for company to Mary in the kitchen, and felt desperately alone.

I had been able to bear it, only because I had hoped that soon I might feel the stirring of a new life within me; but now that hope was dashed. My other consolation had been the belief that Edward loved me, and was simply overburdened with the cares of restoring his home. Now that belief was dashed. Blankness and blackness alone confronted me from now on.

Maria wept too, feeling my sorrow, my hopelessness. She placed my head upon her bosom, and comforted me, as she had sometimes done at Lowood. She attempted to solace me by arguing that I was painting too gloomy a picture:

'There is affection towards you, Jane, I am convinced of that; I see it in his bearing towards you; though I have to confess I have been puzzled by an apparent want of ardour. However, I suspect, as I have said, a purely medical reason for his lack of passion. He is, after all, not in the first flush of youth; and his terrible accident may also have something to do with it. He may well be *ashamed*: have you considered that possibility? He cannot face you because of shame: that is my belief.'

Her reasoning did give me a scintilla of hope. Edward was a proud man; if his accident had in some way affected his virility – a defect that he would only have discovered on our wedding night – he must have endured an agony of shame! It would, indeed, have given him reason to avoid me, both by day and night.

I must talk to him. And – supposing there could be no medical cure – so long as *love* existed, I could endure childlessness. I could pour my maternal feelings into caring for Adèle, during her holidays; and, now that Maria and I were such good friends, I could become, in time, a kind of aunt to her little son.

I ended the day in somewhat better spirits than I had begun it. Edward arrived home late from his business meeting, but drank a tumbler of brandy with us; was warm towards my friend; came to bed at the same time as I, and kissed me goodnight tenderly. He held me lightly round my waist as we said goodbye, the next morning, to Maria. John would take her in the chaise to the inn where she would await the coach to Bradford.

'You must come to see us,' Maria said, her eyes moist – I knew for pity of me.

'We shall!' Edward said. 'And you must visit us, with your husband and son, when we are settled in Thornfield Hall. You've done Jane a power of good! Thank you!'

After one last embrace between the two of us, Maria sped away. Soon Edward was gone too, on the back of Bessie. I felt lonely and fearful. It would take all my courage to confront him, but it had to be done.

''Twere well it were done quickly ...' I thought; and plunged in after dinner, as he relaxed over a cigar. I assured him of my love and devotion; of my understanding of the physical and mental difficulties he had faced after his heroic attempt to save the life of 'that crazed woman'. He listened intently but impassively. I told him how precious to me were our embraces; yet I knew that they lacked 'one essential act'. For want of it I could not produce an heir for him; and that distressed me. I urged him to be open with me; not to feel ashamed or embarrassed. Did he not love me? Or was there another reason?

Taking regular draws on his cigar, he gazed distantly over my shoulder. I waited for his response, but he did not speak. Had he become angry with me, I could have borne it; instead, his face became like stone; entirely blank; and then, such a desolate, despairing look came into it, as I had not seen even when I first stole upon my blinded, crippled master, bearing a glass of water.

'Speak to me, dear Edward!' I pleaded. 'I am sorry if I have distressed you.'

He stood up slowly; stubbed out the half-smoked cigar; moved like a sleepwalker past me and out the door. I heard the outside door open and slam shut; I saw him, through the window, pass slowly. I sat on, frozen. I heard faintly the clop of Bessie's hooves, moving away, fading into silence.

Mary, coming in to clear the dishes, exclaimed: 'Goodness gracious, ma'am, whatever is the matter? Have you got a fever?', because I had started to shake violently, and my teeth were chattering. 'Let me get you up to your bed,' she said, putting her stout, motherly arms around me and helping me to my feet.

'Thank you, Mary,' I said faintly. I knew it was no fever, but wished for nothing more than to lie on my bed. Once in the bed-chamber, she helped remove my clothes and tucked me in, promising to come back with drinks and a hot-water jar.

The hours passed timelessly, as perhaps they do on the Day of Judgement. I did not know which was worse: the cool passivity with which he had listened to my heartfelt words, or the look of blank despair as he got up to leave the room. Neither, I decided. Rather, it was the moment dividing those two states, when – I now realised – he had glared at me with a look of pure, malignant hatred.

My shaking subsided; I drowsed fitfully; Mary came several times, asking if I would like some food. I said no. The late darkness fell. He had not returned – he had abandoned me! Then, sometime in the early hours, when I was neither asleep nor awake, I heard the clip-clop of a horse; and I felt relief and fear together. At least he was safe, he was home. I determined to make myself wake up to confront him; but the fear, I suppose, chose that moment to cast me down into sleep. I dreamed I was being pursued by snakes and scorpions.

Then I was being shaken gently. Mary's face was bending over me, anxiety written all over her wrinkles. I saw light through the curtains. 'Ma'am, ma'am, I thought I should waken you, though

I'm loath to do it with such a message. Bessie come home sometime in the night. But no Master Edward. John found the horse standin' in the yard, when he got up just five minutes since.'

I struggled up in bed. 'Oh, gracious heavens! he's fallen somewhere; is injured! We must find him!'

'Now, don't you worry too much, Jane my dear. I'm sure he's just had a slight fall, and Bessie dashed off. Master Edward is probably makin' his way home on foot. John has gone to rouse Mr Cartwright and they and the other men'll find him in no time.'

'Pass me my stays, my dress, Mary. I must go out and look too.'

She persuaded me I would do much better to leave the searching to the men, who knew what they were doing; knew the paths Edward was used to travelling on.

I came downstairs, took some tea, and paced around the house and yard in a torment. An hour, two hours, went by. I was in the kitchen with Mary, attempting to dull my mind with household activity, when we heard the tramp of boots. I flew out, closely followed by Mary. Mr Cartwright, the farm manager, leading the band of red-faced, perspiring farm-hands – for the day was hot and close – shook his head at me. 'Sorry, Mrs Rochester, we've not found the master yet. But we'll go out further afield after we've had a glass of cider and some bread and cheese, perhaps.'

'Of course – please all go in and sit down.'

Some while later when, for a moment, only Mr Cartwright, John, Mary and myself were in the kitchen, I ventured in a faint voice: 'Mr Cartwright, I think if you don't come across him soon we must think of dragging Graves' Pool.'

He lifted his grizzled, weather-beaten face, startled: 'Mr Rochester would never have taken a fall there; he's too canny; he knows its dangers too well.'

'I was thinking that he might have gone into it … voluntarily. He has been overburdened and low in spirits lately.'

'Master Edward would *nivver* think of takin' his life!' John burst out; and Mary echoed the sentiment with 'Nivver! 'Tis a sin even to think of such a thing!'

I confessed to them how, by chance, I had overheard them make a remark about Graves' Pool, and Mr Rochester, which had strongly implied that he had, during the months following his accident, made a suicide attempt. I quoted their very words. They looked at one another, then at me, and told me firmly I was wrong. Whatever I thought I had overheard, it was not that. The master was a very religious person.

Nevertheless, I persisted, I wanted the pool dragged. The farm manager said it would not be easy, and he was sure there was no need. He, too, knew Mr Rochester, well enough to dismiss such a grim thought. They would go out again at once; widen the search; and they would find him – and find him alive.

I remembered my first sight and sound of Edward: prostrate in the moonlit lane, swearing at his fall; my first words to him: 'Are you injured, sir? … Can I do anything?' And his first words to me: 'Thank you; I shall do: I have no broken bones …' The dark face, the stern features, the heavy brow. I prayed to God this time it would be no worse. Perhaps he had driven far; been too dazed to set off for the farm immediately; or had broken a leg and was forced to wait for someone to find him.

There was another two hours or so of anguished waiting for me; then, again, we heard sounds approaching. I rushed to the door again: and saw the plodding men, their hats in their hands, their heads lowered; a farm-horse drawing a cart, on which – I saw as I rushed to it – lay a human figure covered in a sheet, as if already in a shroud.

5

HE HAD DIED – instantly, one hoped – of a broken neck. They had found him in a gully, some ten miles from the farm. It could only be assumed that Bessie had balked at sudden danger, and thrown her master. He had probably been riding at speed, over unfamiliar ground.

In those first minutes, hours, days, I felt as crazy as his first wife. I do not remember being put to bed by Mary – the doctor arriving and giving me a sedative – nor when I woke from that sleep to the dreadful grief and even more dreadful guilt. I was preserved by the arrival – she assures me it was the following afternoon – of Maria, accompanied this time by her brother-in-law, Mr Jenkins. Maria informed me that, around the time of my discovery of Edward's death, she had experienced a premonition that something was terribly awry at our farm. Her agitation had been such that her brother-in-law, a stout, somewhat ugly, yet altogether kindly, lawyer, had insisted he should drive her here to see me. They both put themselves fully at my service for as many days as I needed them, having at once seen I was in no state to cope with any affairs.

I must at some point have requested Mr Jenkins to look through Edward's papers, though I do not recall doing so; and asked him to seek a meeting with my husband's lawyer. I know that I was grateful for this beneficent stranger's energetic efforts on my behalf. I was calm enough, and lucid enough – one evening when rain lashed the window while I took my last leave of Edward's

51

stony, grim face – for him to draw me aside after, and present me with his findings. His face was grave and compassionate. Edward's financial affairs, he said, were in an appalling state. There were large sums owing to the architect and builders working on Thornfield Hall. To Mr Jenkins' astonishment, there appeared to be no will. Edward's aged uncle, a gentleman who lived in France and whom Edward had not seen in years, would no doubt expect to inherit most of the estate – once the long procedure had been gone through, and the debts paid off. I would be fortunate if, at the end of it, I had enough to live on. My own inheritance, which had been given over to Edward on marriage, had also been lost in the bricks and mortar of a half-finished manor-house.

All this was confirmed, in due course, by Mr Smith, Edward's own lawyer. He claimed that he had persistently tried to persuade his client to make a will, but he had always put the subject off. He had set up trusts for Bertha, many years since, and for Adèle, his ward. She, at least, would be modestly provided for.

'There *is* wealth, Mrs Rochester,' the lawyer said to me, 'but it is tied up in the West Indies. You may be entitled to a small proportion of it. However, in the absence of an heir, probate will take many years, and the outcome, even then, is uncertain. I am sorry.'

At the time, I cared little about these problems. I could think only that my beloved husband was dead, and I had killed him, by too suddenly and crudely calling his attention to a matter that must have hugely threatened his pride as a man. I wept, or I slept, under sedation: little else.

I knew there was one painful duty that I ought not to avoid – the task of breaking the news to Adèle. To my shame, I felt unable to fulfil even this responsibility, but left it to Maria. She and the farm manager drove to the school and, in the headmistress's study, gave the news to the child. By Maria's account, Adèle took it bravely; did not cry; and agreed that it was better if she remained at the school, where she had teachers and friends who would comfort her.

And so it came to the day of the funeral.

Rain had been falling almost constantly for two days: a fitting accompaniment to my feelings, as well as a more characteristic feature of early summer, in these northerly climes, than the heat which had preceded it; but on this day the rain ceased, and the cloud-cover dispersed a little, letting down some watery sunshine. I cannot tell you much about the funeral service, save that the little church – where once we had been almost-married, and once married – was crowded with a mixture of common people and some gentry who had come from far, and I surprised myself by being dry-eyed. I listened to the vicar extolling the dead man as a fine father, husband, master, member of the community, and Christian; listened to him saying that this good man was now in the heavenly mansion. I believed fervently in the justice of the words of praise, yet found it hard to believe in the words of faith. For the first time, that ringing affirmation, 'I am the resurrection and the life', struck me as an unlikely hope.

In the little churchyard, overstocked with ancient and modern graves, I could believe in 'ashes to ashes, dust to dust', but there it ended. My gaze fell on a century-old, mouldered gravestone, bearing the name William Surbiton, his wife Esther and two of their children, and I deemed it most unlikely that this long-dead family were disporting themselves in heaven. My sudden infidelity would have shocked me, no doubt, had I been capable of further shock; but my mind felt numb.

Maria's arm supported me as the coffin was lowered and the earth fell on it. Her Christian murmurs held the full ring of conviction, of entire faith. I wondered how she could be so certain of the life beyond; and how Helen, my childhood friend whom we had both loved, could have been so certain that her failing little body would one day be resurrected in full health and in the joy of the sight of God. Was Helen alive? I did not think so. Today's birds sang; that was the most one could say.

As my friends gently started to guide me away from the grave, a female figure, at the edge of the mourners, turning away and starting to walk off, attracted my attention – to the extent of jolting me out of my dismal state. She seemed familiar – and in some disturbing way. Surely there could be only one woman with that straight red hair under her bonnet; that severe, square-set face, that staid walk? I murmured to my friends, 'Excuse me; there's someone I must speak to; I will catch you up,' and hurried after the departing woman. The staid walk had quickened perceptibly. Two or three people attempted to interrupt my pursuit, offering me condolence, but I brushed them aside, I hoped politely. I was past the lich-gate, and saw her already quite a distance along the church lane. Picking my skirts up, I almost ran after her. She turned her head, and I knew that I had indeed recognised her. She kept on walking, a little more slowly. She stopped and turned altogether as I neared her.

'Grace,' I said, breathing heavily; 'Grace Poole, isn't it?'

'Yes, miss – madam, I should say.'

'Grace, I thought you were dead. I thought you had perished in the fire.'

'No, madam; master saved my life.' I noticed that her eyes were swollen and red.

'Well, that is one blessing, amid all the calamities.'

'I am truly sorry for you,' she said, 'truly sorry.'

'Thank you.'

She nodded, started to turn. 'I must get home. Georgie, my son, will be home from the factory and expecting his supper.'

Though I had never, in earlier times, had any desire to speak

54

with a woman who seemed both taciturn and the very opposite of her name – graceless – now I felt an urgent wish to talk with her – to discover – to explore the past. I told her so; she said, 'There are things best left in the past, Mrs Rochester,' and would not be stayed.

I lingered for a few moments in the lane, then with slow and dreary steps turned back. I found Maria and Mr Jenkins waiting for me by the lich-gate. I was grateful that neither expressed any curiosity, but simply took me by the arms and led me the short distance to the road, where John was waiting for us, to be driven home. I myself broke our silence to say, 'That was one of the servants at Thornfield Hall – Grace Poole. She looked after Bertha Mason. I had thought her dead from the fire; but I find that Edward rescued her.'

'The woman who did not look after her charge very efficiently; who sometimes became the worse for drink, to the danger of you and everyone else?' Maria asked.

'The very same.'

Her brother-in-law remarked that he would not be surprised if she had drunk a pot or two of porter already today, for he had seen her stumble and almost fall, on her way out of the churchyard.

'She is a hard woman,' I said; 'but she was almost a prisoner herself for ten years, shut up with a madwoman.'

Maria shuddered, saying that was indeed a terrible fate. That was true; yet surely no worse than the prison I felt myself bound in, especially when, on the morrow, I said goodbye to Maria and her kind-hearted brother-in-law. I was in a prison of overwhelming grief, guilt, and loneliness. My only relief was to be by myself, thinking of Edward, seeing him everywhere; and yet this was also my great torture.

I forced myself to write letters: to Adèle; to Mr Mason, Edward's brother-in-law in Funchal; to Mrs Fairfax; to St John; to

Mary and Diana. These once-dear companions of mine might be on the high seas, for all I knew, heading for India. They had receded from me, in any case; put themselves at a distance, no doubt blaming me for my 'kindness' in sharing my inheritance with them, and thus depriving their lives of a purpose, miserable though their work might have seemed.

Even the servants, Mary and John, seemed distant, following the funeral; as if they did not know what to say by way of comfort. For two weeks I talked with no one, save Edward's lawyer and agent, whose gloomy countenances matched the news of financial chaos which they had to impart. Was I to be forced to become Jane Eyre, governess, once more?

I took to my bed for days on end; even though the weather had turned fine again, and Mary fussed me that I should dress and enjoy the sunshine, I felt there was no earthly reason why I should leave the bed. If I tried to stir myself to rise, some dead weight pressed upon me, physically preventing me from doing so. I longed for some mortal illness which would carry me off – into nothingness; for I still carried the awful burden of the lack of faith which had fallen on me at the funeral service. My Heavenly Father was dead; as dead as that earthly father who had passed away only months after my birth. If only the typhus, which had carried off him and my mother, would come to me!

One Sunday morning – I knew it was the sabbath, because Mary had flung open my window and I could faintly hear church bells – I heard Edward's voice calling my name, as he had called it once before. 'Jane! Jane! Jane!' 'I'm coming,' I murmured aloud; got up straight away; dressed myself with great care, choosing a gown which he had bought for me just prior to our wedding. Mary pressed her hands together in relief and pleasure as I descended the stairs. 'Thank the Lord, ma'am, you're up! And lookin' as pretty as a picture! I'll fetch your hat and gloves!' I told her I would not be needing them; I was not going to church, I was going for a long walk. The kindly woman said being out in the fresh air, on such a lovely day, would do me just as much good, if not more.

I walked across the fields, to the edge of the dark woods, and entered. The sun was blotted out. I followed the voice – still calling me from time to time. I came out of the trees to the murky stillness of a pool. I had known he would call me to this place, and I was glad of it. How dirty I was! Like the murky pool itself. How base my nature, for having craved more than I had any right to, those nights when he left me unsatisfied! I had even – my God – resorted to a practice which the most vulgar of maidservants would despise! There was a word – John Reed had spoken it to my face when he exposed himself to me, and that had lived on somewhere in me; I'd whispered it on many a solitary night since my marriage, craving whatever it betokened. I was corrupt and depraved.

I started to wade in: with a gasp as the icy-cold water surged up under my skirts. I had waded almost up to my waist, when I found my body gripped from behind, preventing me from proceeding. 'Don't stop me!' I cried out. 'Leave me be!' I did not know who was behind me, his arms around my waist, slowly dragging me back; a wood-cutter, perhaps; or one of our farm-workers; a strong man certainly, against whom my struggles to stay in the pool were vain.

A voice spoke in my ear: a female voice: 'You mustn't do it, ma'am!' The fact that it was a woman's voice somehow unnerved me; I let myself go limp, and she pulled me back onto muddy ground. She and I lay panting. I saw it was Grace Poole. When I had caught my breath I said to her: 'You are very strong, Grace.'

'I had to be, managing Bertha.'

We both sat up. 'Such a fine dress,' she said, 'and look what you've done to it.'

'What does a dress matter?'

'It would matter if you were poor.'

'I am well rebuked.'

She said I should get myself off home quickly; and when I burst into tears and said I did not want to go there, she took a handkerchief from the pocket of her brown stuff dress, for me to wipe my eyes. 'There's a sunny, grassy little spot not far away,' she said. 'We can sit and dry ourselves off.'

My hard-faced saviour helped me to my feet and led the way. We came to a small clearing bathed in sunshine, and sat side by side on a pile of logs. We spread out our skirts to dry.

'What were you doing here?' I asked. 'Do you live nearby?'

'No, ma'am; I live many miles away.' She hesitated, rubbing her hands together, then plunged on: 'My son Georgie drowned here, fourteen year ago. Six years old he was. I was picking blackberries. I let him go off in the care of an older boy; they were playing with a ball. The ball went in the water, and Georgie went in after it. His little legs got stuck in the mud that's on the bottom. He thrashed about in the water, but the more he struggled to get out, the deeper he was drawn in. The other boy ran to fetch me, but by the time I got here it was too late.'

She had uttered this in a steady, emotionless voice, while staring at a butterfly that had settled on a log. 'Oh, Grace!' I said, clasping her hand.

'Well, it's a long time ago. But I like to come here and sit by the water sometimes – since the Hall burnt down.'

'Georgie ... But you said, after Mr Rochester's funeral, he would be expecting his supper.'

She smiled slightly, in a way that was more like a grimace of pain, and said, 'Sometimes I make up stories. He would be twenty now.'

She told me it offended her that I had walked into the pool, presumably intending to end my life, when her son had so wanted to live. I accepted this second rebuke by declining my head.

'And your husband?' I asked. 'Did he blame you for your son's death?'

'There was no husband.'

'Oh, I see.'

'Do you, ma'am?' – an ironic look in her eyes.

I didn't answer. I closed my eyes, my face raised to the sun's warmth; and began to feel almost glad that Grace had saved me. 'Thank you for pulling me out,' I said.

'I know what grief is. I felt like killing myself when –' she nodded in the direction of the pool. 'But I didn't have the strength to do it, I suppose. Instead I drank. And, to pay for it, I went to work in Grimsby.'

'At the asylum.'

She laughed harshly. 'No, ma'am! I've never been in an asylum in my life. I worked the docks.'

I did not understand. 'You were a porter?'

'I was a whore.'

The savage word went through me, as icily as the pool water had done. She went on: 'I did that for four years; and then Mr Rochester – found me. He said he had a wife who had gone mad, and would I look after her. So I have master to thank for rescuing me from a life of sin.' Her look, as she spoke this, registered gratitude – but also something else, something that looked more like the irony I had observed earlier. And suddenly she stood up, announcing: 'Well, 'tis time I was going home. Our clothes are dry enough.'

Standing up too – and suddenly giddy from all that had occurred and been revealed – I clutched at her shoulder for support. 'Grace,' I said, 'can I talk to you again? Will you come and take tea with me sometime soon? I need to talk – oh, I need so much to talk!'

'I reckon you do. All right.'

We agreed a day in the coming week; then we walked one behind the other through the trees until our paths separated.

When, three or four days later, Grace was shown into the parlour to join me for tea, she remarked in her dry manner that she was glad to see me looking better. I did not *feel* much of an amelioration in my looks or spirits; yet the remark compelled me to recognise that I had not continued in that hopeless, suicidal state of the sabbath. I had got up and dressed every day, and tried to busy myself with replying to letters of sympathy. Among the many somewhat formal letters had been a long letter from Diana and Mary, full of heartfelt compassion and warm love.

Diana, the actual scribe, expressed remorse over their not having visited, and having been laggard in correspondence. They could now reveal the reason and plead for forgiveness. They had both, by good fortune and almost simultaneously, formed a reciprocated attachment with two gentlemen of excellent character: Diana, with a captain in the navy, and Mary a clergyman. 'Love, dear sister, has too much occupied our time and thoughts.' They were both engaged to be married. They felt sorrow at the contrast between their own sudden happiness and the tragedy which had overwhelmed me. They begged me to pay them a visit.

Their letter warmed me, and I suppressed the emotion of envy. I wrote back my felicitations; said there was nothing to forgive; and felt enabled, because of this renewed intimacy, to pour out some of the problems which were assailing me, such as the ruinous state of Edward's finances.

During these days, between my walk to Graves' Pool and Grace's visit, I had managed to divert some of my grief into an obsessional questioning of her revelation of her past life. I kept wondering and imagining how my husband had 'found' her. It scarcely bore thinking of; yet my most lurid imaginings were much less agonising than grief for his death. He had told me a mistruth; yet I could forgive him that. Delicacy, towards both myself and Grace, had made a white lie seemly. What I could not understand was why he had chosen such a woman to look after Bertha.

It was one of my first questions to Grace, after I had poured the tea and we had got through the first polite nothings. I phrased it tactfully: why had he chosen her, when she had had no experience of looking after mad people?

She cooled the hot tea in her saucer before replying. 'Mrs Rochester – Bertha – could be very foul-mouthed, ma'am. She couldn't help it, poor soul; it was part of her sickness. I was used to such language; the men I went with weren't exactly refined ...' – that slight, ironic smile – 'and he could see I was a strong young woman.'

It seemed satisfactory. I asked her to call me 'Jane', not ma'am. 'You're not my servant, Grace.'

''Twouldn't seem right to call you Jane. Yet Mrs Rochester don't seem right either. How about I call you miss, like before?'

Reminding myself that I was, to all intents, still a spinster, I said, 'Yes, all right.'

'If you're wondering, miss, how we came to meet – he came back with me to my room, but we didn't do anything. He wanted someone to talk to, that was all – like you.'

'About what?'

'This and that. His poor mad wife, that he'd brought back from abroad, mostly.'

The parlour door, left ajar, was pushed open, and Pilot snuffled in. He had been moping and miserable; yet on sight of Grace he wagged his tail and rushed towards her. 'How are you, Pilot?' she said. 'Grieving for master like the rest of us, I expect.' Crouching at her feet, leaning his head up for her stroke, he continued to wag his tail. I was surprised, for Grace had always generally kept to her and Bertha's room, not mixing with the other servants.

'She remembers you!' I observed; 'she remembers you from Thornfield!'

'I've seen her since then, often.'

'Oh, how was that?'

'I used to visit master here, before you came, miss.'

My surprise increased; besides a slight discomfiture. It explained why she and Mary had exchanged familiar greetings – cool-sounding on the latter's part, a curt 'Grace' and a nod.

'That was kind of you.'

'As I said, he liked to talk.' She glanced around: 'You've changed the curtains; and the cushion covers. The room is brighter.' And we talked about furnishings for a few minutes, during which interval I had not the least idea what she said or what I said, for into my mind had flashed a thought: *'That* was what I overheard Mary say! Not Graves' Pool but *Grace Poole*! "'Tis better for'n than Grace Poole."

Master had been generous to her, she said; and she had been able to save most of her wages over the years. She could get by, if she was careful; but time hung heavy on her. Still, I pointed out, she must find her life easier than when she had looked after Bertha Mason: 'I can't imagine how you could endure it, Grace. For ten years, to be locked away with a depraved, violent madwoman. Intolerable!'

'You gets used to it. And Bertha was not always mad. Sometimes she'd be quite sane, quite like you and me, for weeks on end; and in those times she could be good company. She got much worse in the last year or so. Until then, she never got free or attacked anybody.'

I knew that to be true, as it corresponded with Edward's account, following our aborted wedding.

She stooped in her chair to stroke Pilot again. The dog, almost asleep, started slightly. 'She could be a very intelligent woman, miss, when she was in her right mind. I'm not stupid, but I'm not bright either. I couldn't talk to her about books and pictures and such like, yet we had women's things in common. We both knew what it feels like to lose a precious son.' Glancing up from her stroking, seeing my look of shock, she burst out: 'Oh, miss, don't tell me master never told you they had a son!'

'No. He didn't tell me that,' I said faintly.

'Oh, miss, I'm sorry! I never thought he would keep anything from you, his wife!'

Asked to tell me what she knew, she said there had been a son called Robert, somewhere a long way off, in the Indies – under my coaxing she agreed it could have been an island called Martinique, in the West Indies. Master had left him behind with Bertha's family when he brought her to England. Bertha, in her sane times, grieved for him a lot.

'Did Mr Rochester confirm this to you?' I asked, hoping it was a mere delusion of a diseased brain.

'Yes.'

She said she had better go; I looked as if I could do with some peace and quiet; and I did not try to dissuade her, only asking her at the door if she would come again, and she said she would if I wanted it.

She had given me much to make my days restless and my nights void of sleep. But why should I believe a common whore? Would not Edward have told me? By the time Grace came again, I had decided to put no faith in her wild story. I thought rather that – perhaps out of thwarted love for 'master' – she was attempting to provoke me.

I had heard the expression *in vino veritas*, and I decided to put it to the test. The day was a hot, breathless one; she came at midday, when the sun was beating down. I asked Mary to bring us a pitcher of cider, which she did disapprovingly, aware of Grace's failing.

Her coarse face became even coarser, and empurpled, as she gulped the cider. I ordered the pitcher to be refilled. In the face of my cajolings and insinuations, she revealed that Mr Rochester had sometimes visited her poor cottage, once his sight was sufficiently restored for him to ride. 'Just for a chat, I assure you.' She hiccuped. 'Master never laid a finger on me, ever. He was a good man, a faithful man. I'd bet a pound to a penny, he never – went with – any woman other than Bertha and yourself.'

I opened my mouth to say that was palpably untrue, there had been at least three mistresses on the continent, during his desperate, immoral years; and there was Adèle to testify to it. I even uttered the words, 'You are incorrect, because ...' I stopped short. It would have wronged his memory to have mentioned mistresses, and she would have assumed Adèle was his ward. He himself had disputed his fatherhood of her; though no one observing the cast of the child's lips and brow as she frowned and pouted could have doubted she was his daughter.

In the mood for a bitter revelation of my own, I continued, after a hiatus: '... because our marriage was – not consummated.' A heavy sigh, almost a groan, burst from me.

Betraying no surprise, she murmured, 'So he only went with Bertha. He loved you, I'm sure of that; but I don't think you were right for each other, miss.'

'Evidently.'

There was nothing else of interest. I could not conceive how Edward could have found her company desirable. When the second pitcher was drained, and she staggered to her feet, she said, 'I brought something to show you, miss.' She had a basket with her, full of simple provisions that she proposed giving to a housebound friend, an old woman, on her way home. She fumbled under the provisions and brought out a package, handing it to me, saying she had found it in the still-smouldering ruins of Thornfield Hall. 'There were a few other things I found, but I saved them to give to master; but I kept this, for it was mine, as you will see.'

I drew out from the packet a sheet of drawing-paper, charred along the edges and somewhat curled up. I saw on it a sketch, in charcoal, of a handsome-looking young woman in an elegant dress and broad-brimmed hat, holding on her lap a curly-haired infant. The two figures were on a veranda; the skilful artist had sketched lightly, about the figures, what seemed to be tropical plants and flowers.

'Look on the other side,' Grace instructed me. I turned it over; saw, written in a bold masculine hand, '*Artiste: Claude Signoret, St Pierre, 1822*'; underneath this, more gracefully, femininely: 'To dear Grace, from her grateful mistress, Bertha Rochester.'

Replacing the drawing carefully in the packet, I returned it to her. 'I treasure this,' she said. 'Bertha had six drawings of herself and her son. Two others were only a little spoiled, like this, and I gave them to master; only of course he couldn't see them.' She put the package back under the provisions. 'What I'd give, miss, for a drawing of Georgie!' I thought she would cry; but she held back her tears. Moved – as well as certain now that she had told me the truth – I embraced her.

The lonely days passed. A dozen instruments of torture were at work inside my skull. I summoned Mr Smith and asked him frankly if Edward had ever referred to a son on the island of Martinique. He poured scorn on the very idea. I wrote to Mr Mason, Bertha's brother. A reply came: yes, there was a son, Robert; the family plantation had passed into other hands, but his understanding was that Robert was somewhere on the island. His exact whereabouts were unknown. He would now be about twenty.

Slowly, in my solitude, my despair, my grief – yes, and anger too, that Edward had found me so lacking in attraction – an outrageous idea took hold; nothing less than to sail for the West Indies and try to find Edward's son. I scarcely knew my motives for what became, over a few weeks, an obsession. There were, it is true, financial incentives. Mr Smith – as astonished as I – confirmed that if my husband truly had a living son, the legal process of sorting out the estate would be incomparably simpler and more swift; and I would be likely entitled to a modest but sufficient portion. Yet this weighed with me much less than other, intangible factors.

Those kept changing from day to day. One day, I felt that finding his son would bring Edward alive to me again; the next, that he would be the offspring of Bertha Mason too, and it would be dreadful, yet altogether not to be avoided! Another day, that I might find Prospero's enchanted island; the next day, that I would at least escape my miserable life by, most probably, being drowned on the voyage, or murdered on the island by some savage runaway slave.

Another day I would dream, like Ariel, like Caliban, of freedom.

For all these reasons, I became obsessed with sailing towards the setting sun. But I had no money. It was as much as I could do to pay the wages at the farm. Work on Thornfield had ceased, and enormous bills piled up in Edward's study. Yet Providence – once again in the form of Diana and Mary – took a hand. Enclosing a bankers' note for two thousand pounds, they wrote that they had no need of all the money I had generously provided for them; they were to be married shortly and would be well taken care of. This partial return, they hoped, would be useful to me; they would be insulted if I returned it.

It decided me.

When next Grace Poole called to see me, I said to her, 'How would you like to come with me to Martinique, Grace?' Amused at her bewilderment, I explained my intentions. After thinking for only a few moments, she said she had nothing to keep her here; but why did I choose to ask her, of all people, to be my servant?

'I'm not asking you to be my servant, Grace; though of course I would not expect you to undertake it without recompense; but I wish you to come as my companion. I have no friend who would be free to go with me on such a long expedition. Besides, you must have learned something about those islands, and the ways of their people, from Bertha.'

'A little, I suppose.'

'And indeed we have become more than acquaintances, have we not?'

She smiled and nodded – the first time I had seen her smile with some warmth.

I set about arranging our voyage; bought us both suitable clothes for the tropics; left all in the hands of Edward's agent. On a morning of good, sweet English rain, we crossed the English Channel to Calais, the first stage of our long journey to Martinique.

Martinique, French West Indies 1999

6

SOON AFTER ARRIVAL on the island, I was sitting at a table opposite a plain, bespectacled Martinique girl nervously checking a list. 'Charlotte Brontë?' she asked, and I nodded. She made a tick on her paper and said with a warm smile, 'Welcome to our beautiful island, Madame Brontë.'

'*Merci.*'

'Your coach will be along very soon.'

You may imagine, briefly, a large room with whirling fans, in which several tired ladies, aged from thirty to seventy, are confronting across small tables the same number of Martinique girls, armed with lists and pens; another girl circulates with a tray containing glasses and a jug of fruit juice. My own nervous girl, who has made the understandable error over my name, says she has been given the honour of helping me in any way I wish; to be my guide, for example. She writes on a sheet of paper and gives it to me. 'Please, don't hesitate, Madame Brontë. My name is Marie.' I thank her.

At the end of such an immense journey, the dreamy, drowsy coach-ride seemed interminable.

We arrived at the hotel assigned to us. The night was clammy, wrapping us as in a shroud. The hotel proved to be not one building but several, composing a circle. Moonlit waters gleamed: we were on the edge of a bay; straight across from us was Martinique's capital. I signed my name, 'Charlotte Brontë'; then we followed a porter to our accommodation, assailed as we walked by a constant chorus of small creatures, sounding like maracas or castanets. The noise seemed an aural embodiment of the stifling heat.

Our room, at least, was cool, with french windows opening to a ground-floor terrace, and the bay beyond. We sat out on the terrace. While we had unpacked, clouds had obscured the moon. I felt a drop or two of welcome rain. Palm trees rustled suddenly, and the heat eased just a fraction from one second to the next. Suddenly, the sky fell in sheets. We bathed ourselves in the rain, then went inside and got ready for bed.

I woke at five-thirty. The room had become warm and stale during the night, and the washed, clear dawn sky beyond the window looked temptingly cool; but when I stepped outside in my robe, the heat hit me like a physical blow. Nonetheless, I sat there for a while, thinking of my life at home.

And my sombre reflections continued, even while I was drinking juice and coffee in the restaurant, exchanging small talk with my temporary companion. I knew I was incomparably privileged, compared with most people; and yet I was inconsolably lonely. The tiny baby crab, crawling on the patio outside, was not lonelier than I.

I thought of that grey, storm-buffeted rectory, with people passing each other like ghosts: stern Emily, cheerful Anne, compulsive Branwell, aloof Patrick, Aunt Branwell clucking in her Cornish dialect, the servants – all alone. The girls quietly embroidering their brief lives. And all of them – all of us – crying into the void, 'Jane! Jane! Jane!' or something similar.

And sometimes we wanted to call out to the dead; as Charlotte – as I – wanted to call out to the mother; but we didn't know where they were, and they didn't answer.

Several hours later, after an abortive ferry-ride across the bay to

Fort de France – everything was closed for 'Liberation of the Slaves' – and some other exploration, I was lying on the bed with Jerry, a beach waiter. I love to talk during sex, and this time I chose to lapse into my mother's lyrical Cornish, which she never lost despite marriage to an up-country 'toff' and mixing in his bookish circles. 'That's right, fuck me, my 'andsome! Get it right in there ... Bite my neck, my breasts, my lover ... I d'like that ...' and so on. He was frowning, not understanding, and I had to show him. At that moment my bedside phone rang. I could have left it, but there is always that fear that something bad has happened, so I picked up the phone. It was my husband.

Jerry slid from me, but I kept him interested by finding his anus with my toe, while talking to David. I kept something of the singsong in my voice as we discussed the weather (theirs cool and damp, ours unbearably hot), our cleaning lady's inadequate ironing, how much rent we should ask for the spare bedroom, Jeremy's late nights with the computer, and so on. He said, 'Your voice sounds funny.' It didn't seem funny to me, I replied; it was probably the long distance.

'Anyway I'll have to go, darling, I'm being interviewed; kiss the children for me. I'll give you a call in a couple of days ... I miss you too.' I slid my toes up to his velvety black cock, gently stroking. David said Alison wished to speak to me, and put her on. She demanded a new riding outfit; her present one made her feel ashamed, when compared with Imogen Hunter's. I pulled his body close and licked his nipple. I pointed out that Imogen's dad was a merchant banker, we didn't have the money to go to Harrods, and it was time she was in bed. I told her I loved her and she rang off, grumbling. I guided Jerry into me again.

From somewhere near the ceiling I looked down at our en-twined bodies, distantly, with amusement. It's said that newly-dead people do this – look down at their corpses. The difference was, I wasn't newly dead; I died a long time ago.

I have drowned. I am underwater. I am *Das Boot*. I am looking for long black bodies like Jerry's to sink my torpedoes into.

When he had come in me he got up to visit the bathroom and I clicked off the cassette recorder nestling among the books and phone by my bedside.

Padding back, tall, ebony, gleaming, solemn, Jerry pulled on his blue shorts and sat on the bed. It had been good, he said, stroking my arm. But why did I want to be bitten? He didn't like biting a woman. It was not decent. Women should be respected. Besides, he could get into trouble if I made a complaint.

'I'm not going to. I asked you to do it.'

He nodded towards the phone. *'Votre mari?'*

'Non, mon père. Il est vieux; je demeure seule avec lui.'

I'd rung him on arrival, and he'd sounded very lonely and down. I worried about him and felt guilty.

'A Londres?'

'Non, en Yorkshire. *C'est au nord.'*

Solemn-faced, he absorbs it like a child learning his lesson. 'Boyfriend?' he asks, using the English word.

I blow out through my lips and shrug, in a Gallic way, and struggle on in my schoolgirl French: *'Il y a un homme qui m'aime; il voulait me marier et j'ai dite oui. Mais j'ai découverte qu'il était déjà marié. Je l'ai découverte quand sa femme, qui est folle, tout à fait folle, essaya de me … m'enflammer dans mon lit, avant le mariage.'* I didn't know the word for wedding dress, so I said, *'Robe de mariage, lingerie aussi – tout.'*

The furrowed brow, the solemn protruding negroid lips as he listens and tries to understand. 'This, bad man, Charlotte,' he ventures at last.

Again the puff, the shrug. *'Ah, oui! Mais il ne voulait la ... troubler plus.'*

'I must go now, Charlotte.'

'Yes, I feel sleepy. Thank you. I'll see you.'

He nodded, pulled open the french window, said au revoir and slipped out.

I rested. Thought of my son, Jerry (though David prefers to call him Jeremy), pink and freckled, with eyes so blue they were virtually colourless and this man Jerry who felt dark, so that if I were to cut through him like a tree, he would be dark all the way through. Just thinking about him made me feel wet again and I lay across the bed on the damp, rucked-up sheets and found my own fingers entering my cunt and drawing out the long egg-white-like semen – I stroked my fingers beneath my nostrils, expecting somehow to smell spice or the sweetness of rum, but it had the same clean pollen smell of my husband's sperm, a dull smell. Yawning and stretching, I went into the small shower room, catching Jerry's scent again on my hair.

Refreshed, newly virginal, and a creature of impulse, I decided I would surprise and please David by writing him a letter; a long, descriptive, affectionate letter. To make up for the beach boy. I didn't make a habit of screwing other men, and I certainly hadn't come here wanting or expecting to 'pull'. I found some hotel notepaper and settled at a small desk.

My dearest David,

I just talked to you briefly across the great waters but had to cut it short because of an interview. Hearing your sweet voice, even though you sounded tired – and no wonder, having to deal with our two juvenile delinquents! – makes me want to reach out. I'd ring, but you're probably in bed already. It would be lovely to be there with you; we don't make love enough these days, we need to make space and energy for it.

The flight from Charles de Gaulle was packed, and I was very glad to be in Club Class. It was pleasant, for an hour, catching up with Yvette's news; she's living with a rich banker guy. She's got quite plump since we saw her in '96, but says Jean-Pierre likes her this way. I don't know how I'll cope with sharing a room with her for a week; it all seems *trop intime* … She sends her regards to you.

I was telling you Fort de France was entirely closed for the holidays – it was rather creepy, a whole city, that might have been in the French provinces, with the shutters down, apart from a few market stalls full of rotting fruit and scrawny chickens. So we caught the ferry back almost at once, and managed to find a hire-car place open. Jolly, busty sales-woman – unusual, because there's not much sense of jollity here, not like Jamaica, though it seems much richer. We drove past 'Hemingway's Bar', up through the village of Trois Ilets – village square, pretty church, tall, mournful youths outside a booze shop. Bosky road, eventually dusty beaches. We stopped for a swim at one called Les Anses. Awful, humid heat!

Perfect beach, though, almost deserted. We walked down between two bars – both scruffy, end of season, one with plastic tables and umbrellas set drunkenly in the sand. Just two couples and a group of black girls, maybe about ten years old, jumping in and out of the gentle surf; boats lining the edge of the bay, clinking and bobbing.

A young black guy appeared from one of the small concrete houses abutting the beach – he'd been sleeping; I could see the bare room, just a low bed and a stool and a piece of cloth covering the window. The first thing that struck me about him was his seriousness – he didn't smile in greeting nor when he brought our beers, icy cold in American-style insulating covers. I watched him as he went back behind the bar, his head loose on his shoulders, his arms long and hands muscled as he wiped the grease along from one side to the other, all the while staring out at the bay. He returned to our table with two small glasses – ti-punch, a tiny thimble full of white rum – that with the heat made me feel dizzy instantly. Yvette was quite taken with him. I think she liked his wide shoulders, long thin legs in faded cotton shorts and his holed T-shirt … We talked for a while; but he was so serious, David, so melancholy! His eyes seemed tired, the whites slightly yellowed. I couldn't imagine him in a steel band! I think there are probably a lot like him; and a lot of chic, leathery Frenchwomen out to sleep with them.

I didn't feel like exposing my pallid body to him, so didn't swim, but Yvette had no such inhibitions. Since there were no other customers and his boss was out fishing, he bummed a lift with us, said he had a girlfriend near here; but I left him and Yvette walking together …

Wish you'd been able to come with me, darling. Our little Clio is air-conditioned and nippy, we could have explored the island together as I don't intend to spend every moment at the Schoelcher … Still, there's Tuscany to look forward to, and we must make it a real holiday, not take our work with us. We must take nice long siestas, making it clear to the kids that we're not to be disturbed!

We should explore some of the fantasies that we started to talk about before my breakdown. Especially the one –

Feeling thirsty and in need of a swim, I break off at that point. I put on my bikini and go out into the hazy yet blinding light, making for the hotel pool. The waiter who serves me a rum cocktail asks me my name and I tell him, 'Charlotte. Charlotte Brontë.' 'You are French?' he asks; and I say no, I'm English. 'I guess you don't get many English women here.'

'Not many. Lots of Canadian women – at least there used to be, but I think they find it very expensive now.'

'Their dollar's fallen, hasn't it?'

'I don't know. We used to get whole plane-loads. I won't tell you what they came for.'

'I can guess.'

I can see his beady eyes sizing me up as not easily shockable. He continues: 'We called them the pussy-flights.'

I spare him a vague, unresponsive smile; ask him if he has visited France. He corrects me – *this* is France, the island is a *département*, but yes, he has worked in Paris for a few months. He liked it, but likes the tropical warmth better. He seizes my lighter to light my cigarette, then moves away to another table.

I had a swim, then went back to the room. The letter I had left on the desk now seemed pointless as well as dishonest; I scrunched it up and tossed it in the waste-basket. I took from my overnight bag the two tattered Humphry Davy Grammar School homework books, twenty years old, and scribbled in one of them for a while. Yvette arrived, interrupting my thoughts, hot and ill-tempered. The Spanish feminist critic she'd arranged to have a drink with had turned up with a bald, unsavoury husband, who claimed to be a male feminist, and who'd monopolised the entire conversation while his wife gazed worshipfully at him.

We walked out of the grounds and made our way to the nearby marina. 'So, tell me all about Jerry!' she said with a giggle, over Creole-style chicken. 'What was he like?' She hadn't been fazed when Jerry had jumped into the back of our car – after all, I'd been married for forever, and she was French. Actually, I replied, I'd only wanted to interview him for a piece I'd promised to MsLexia, a new English women-only mag. Her face fell. What a shame they'd not been able to come, she said: our men; and I replied, Yes, it was, but David's work at the Millennium Dome was simply too demanding, and anyway there were the children. I talked about Alison and Jeremy for a while; she'd met them briefly when she and her then-husband came to Westminster University, and I'd invited them for a meal after her lecture to my students. She'd fallen for our kids, she said.

Exhausted and jetlagged, we could hardly drag ourselves the short distance back to the hotel. The heat was still so crushing it was like wading through the sea. Handing me our key, the receptionist – a solemn-faced guy who'd been on duty when we arrived – said to me in French, 'Have a restful night, Madame Brontë.'

'*Brontë!*' Yvette exclaimed as we emerged from the fan-cooled reception to the dark outdoor sauna once more. I explained the slight error made by the tired, confused girl who'd welcomed me at the airport. 'She got the columns muddled on her sheet. She thought some London *professeur* by the name of Charlotte Brontë was going to be lecturing on some novelist called Miranda Stevenson! I thought I'd go along with it.'

She gave a little yelp of pleasure, saying, 'It is most droll!'

'Well, I feel I know her better than I know myself – though that's not saying a lot.'

Indoors, in the divinely air-conditioned coolness, we hauled off our sweat-soaked shorts and shirts. We were in bed by ten, and awake again soon after five. An early breakfast, and then we were driving out on quiet roads, skirting the southern coast. As I drove through one deserted lane, flanked by cane, I saw the eyes of many infants, on either side, in the ditches. I knew they were aborted children, waiting for their mothers to pass, waiting to take revenge. Yvette, never blessed with conception though she had hopes of her new man, Jean-Pierre, did not see them.

I don't know if my mood jangled her, but she wanted to go back to the hotel and spend the rest of the day by the pool, recovering properly from the flight. I dropped her off and set out again.

7

STILL THINKING of that creepy country road where all the babies had been hiding in the ditches on each side, I drove at random, not knowing or caring where I was headed. I was travelling north from Fort de France, along a wide freeway at first. Few cars were on the road. It was Sunday, and the middle day of the seemingly endless holiday weekend. Moving my body forward against the seatbelt, I began to enjoy the forward thrust of the car, the open road, the speeding. The landscape that flashed by might have been in any warm island – Madeira, say.

The road descended suddenly to a seaside village that was unmistakably Caribbean. Rank vegetation, a blend of growing and rotting; and a line of tall men, like shadows, on the beach, pulling on heavy nets that stretched the length of the shingle. The men seemed ancient, like a carving in a cave from a forgotten civilisation. The net, the village, fish, the ocean, men bringing food ashore, living wholly in their bodies and their strength. And on the other side of the road, women in white, over-fussy frilly dresses and hats were on their way to church. It seemed back to front: it ought to be the men dressed in white, I felt, linking the world with the spiritual, and the women dealing with the chaos of the sea and nature; for their uncontrollable mysterious bodies were much more part of the island and its endlessly growing, seething flora. I drove too fast along the sea front road and one of the men on the beach shook his fist. I raised a finger and then, through my rear-view mirror, saw him lift his forearm in an obscene gesture. It was a picture I knew I would treasure; he was fucking me, seeing me as French, probably, a *métropolitaine*, in my hired car – and he was also fucking France and Europe, that had given him the good roads and unemployment benefit, and in return demanded that he give up only his proud independence and become a slave.

And the tragedy was – it came to me as I tried to fish out and light a Silk Cut one-handed, dangerously mis-steering the car – that he couldn't see any way of *not* being a slave; trapped by the state's benevolence, and the petrol stations and the shopping malls, and the car in almost every family (so my guidebook informed me). The plantation slaves of the last century could rebel, or try to escape, because life was toil and suffering; but there was no escaping from the soft life. They would pull in their net, and squat on the beach, resting against a palm; drink a can of Lorraine, pass around the joint, laugh about the girls they'd fucked.

At a sign pointing to the house of Gauguin, I left the main road. Immediately the foliage closed in around the car, the route grew twisty and steep and the trees tall, some growing straight, some listing across the road. At home, in England, tree-lined roads often have the light gothic grandeur of a cathedral, but here they were dark, sinister, full – I knew – of crawling creatures, their legs spread against flowers that were lush and overstated. The origins of life felt uncomfortably close, life and death, as all this splendid growing depended on the rotting fruit and dying trees: life, a parasite on all the lives that have gone before; my own life, its freedom and convenience predicated on the denial of life, the killing of a soul that had gills like the heaps of gasping fish hauled up onto the beach. He – or she, for I never enquired about the sex – would be just over three, now.

Shit, I had no idea where I was but couldn't stop on these bends to check the map, just keep driving, higher and higher, trying not to lose revs as the road got steeper, no villages or places to stop and I was thirsty. Then a sign, for tourists but who the fuck would be up here in their hire car – 'Serre de Papillons, 2km'. I turned into a lane that descended and ended in a car park with bays marked for several coaches. There were only two other cars. I got out and left the air-conditioning for the heat that felt like a smothering damp blanket, the first trickle of sweat sliding down my back.

All around were the ruins of what looked like factory warehouses. I could hear a low chorus of pain, of slave women being taken from behind like dogs, and men being beaten. I looked up into the wild eyes of a man strung on a tree by his wrists and ankles, bloody streaks showing through a sweat-stained shirt. I cried out in tune with a bird's taking off from the upper branches and the wind blew and the man was just shadows and dark leaves and then the rain came down with a loud whisper that hushed the moaning and blended with the tears that unexpectedly filled my eyes.

I ran the length of the car park and was suddenly in the plastic world of a tourist-conscious France. A jolie madame, immaculately made up, took too much money for a ticket and offered me a colourful guidebook and poster. I drank a Coke; its sugary synthetic flavour appealed more than the over-sweetness of fruit. Jerry had called me, when first stroking my breast, all the Creole names for fruit as well as *doudou*, sweetness; but I'd preferred it when, asked what the Creole word for cunt was, he said *patate* was one of them. Potato. It felt easier to be earthy-solid, not likely to rot in a day, not so full of seeds and sweetness that all the birds want to peck at the flesh and insects crawl inside you.

I went through double doors and was suddenly in a world that felt as if it was in the clouds, a steamy cooling world where gentleness reigned and babies might float by, counting their toes.

And then – well, I'll give it in the words I talked into my tape recorder, in the car, an hour later; in a dreamy voice, the soft Celtic burr so like my mother's, the lilt that's become metropolitanised ... a voice that drifted, rose, fell, settled for a while, like the butterflies in the glasshouse ... 'And then, with a strange flopping motion, a giant morpho fell and rose again in front of my face, it was blue falling like brightness from the sky and all I could think of was the bright blue of the first cot I bought for the nursery when I was big and round and David's hand on my belly was warm. And – it d'sound crazy, I know – but that blue somehow filled me and I felt I could take off with it and float in the fog and land on the leaves, like I'm a leaf, suckin' water from the roots and dropping easily to the ground ... Just like I'm floating now: oh yes! that's so good ...

'That water, I d'feel it from my mouth to my toes, but especially in there where you are, my 'andsome – flowin' around and around like blood. And I did something terrible, not to the morpho, that blue is sacred, sacred like a boy child, that is so precious. Even if the morpho had let me touch its wings, I could never have harmed it. No, the terrible thing I did was to a monarch butterfly that landed on my arm, so trustin', its little antennae lost in the fine blonde hairs just here ... I think I wanted to find out whether it would be blood comin' out and finding instead it was some kind of brown butterfly juice, which I tasted ... some bitter it was! I tore the body from the wings, then used the wings to dust the back of my hands with orange powder. Some butterflies only live for a day and I thought, I'll show them even that can't be relied on ...

'I would never do that to the morpho – seemed more bird than butterfly, more beautiful than any creature I've ever seen. And I loved the cases of chrysalises, like – like they cheap green ear-rings you d'find in Marazion market, all stored up for hatching, like all those small eggs inside me are. I stayed in there for hours, be-

witched by two monarchs fucking on the wing, and wanting to
know how do it feel to be weightless and fucking! And wondering
who, in the butterfly world, fucks who, and whether they ever do
it across the species, orange yearning for blue, like me so white
yearning for blackness – and the spiders in the glass cases were
fantastic, so evil, just like I am between my legs – how does it feel
to go in there, to put your cock into all that darkness ... you don't
understand a word I've said, do you? I love it! – just crazy with
having your *lapin* in my mashed potato ...'

He had said to me, 'I just love that voice, lady ... the white voice
... keep talkin', while I do it ...' And now, when he'd done it, he
said, 'Oh man, that's better'n a song!'

I lifted myself up and askew into the driver's seat, smiling at the
man. His sweat-soaked T-shirt clung to his rounded belly, his limp,
damp penis and balls hung over his pulled-down shorts. I let him
rearrange himself and pull himself up onto the seat before I
reversed the car off the verge and out of the gap in the forest. I'd
seen him at a wayside bus stop, his hands resting on a machete;
obviously a plantation worker. He'd looked so tired and hot I'd
stopped for him. I'd seen his surprise and hesitation: why should
a white, and a woman in particular, take the risk of offering him a
lift?

We had chatted as I drove; he'd spent a couple of years on St
Lucia, and was proud of his English. I'd pulled in, taken his hand
and put it under my skirt. When I dropped him in a little hamlet,
silent and empty except for a few children kicking a ball, he said,
'Lady, I won't forget this trip. My girl, she won't believe it happen,
she'll think I make it up.'

He took two steps away from the car, then stopped and came
back, leaning in: 'I don't know your name,' he said.

'Charlotte.'

'Mine is Luc.'

I drove back, slowly, languidly. I wasn't just seeing all the greens and mauves and golds, I was seeing my mother in all her bewitchingness and her misery. All her flamboyance, the way my father couldn't keep his eyes from the mysteries beyond the hem of her skirt; and hearing her voice, seductive or raging, behind closed doors. At the same time, I was feeling his white stuff trickling down.

Idly as I dreamed-along through the brilliant colours I wondered if I had time to fuck all the men on this island. It would be a way of passing the time, a pleasant alternative to collecting postcards or ethnic dolls. Now I'd begun, I might as well go on. Unleashing the torpedoes underwater.

Of course it wasn't fair on David. Working overtime in London, he'd be rushing frantically around the Dome, that giant pin-cushion in Greenwich, our age's response to, and improvement on, the great but unentertaining medieval cathedrals and Sir Chris Wren's Dome. Seconded by his friend Peter Mandelson from his regular job at Carlton TV, David's remit was to inject fresh ideas. So – just before my departure – he'd had the splendid thought of having a brain-shaped sort of punchbag, in the Body Zone, which would move about and speak jokes in the staccato style of our friend Ben Elton. He'd be obsessed with his work, entirely innocent, before rushing home to relieve a child-sitter ... while I, here ...

Yvette, to my relief, wasn't in our room when I arrived back. I switched on the French news and, while I drank mineral water, saw that NATO had again caused some 'collateral damage' in Serbia: that coy term for children having their legs blown off, or being burnt to a cinder. I felt rage. Clinton and Blair, the benevolent dictators! The righteous ones! The modern crusaders! Warfare against a crime so dreadful – genocide – it was worth killing a few hundred innocent civilians for; yet not worth seriously risking a single NATO life! When I saw Chirac, then Clinton,

84

then Blair, mouthing their pious platitudes, I screamed at them, 'Fuck you! Fuck you! Fuck you!'

I wrote for a while in the old notebook, taking on the story that I'd been writing – continuing, rather – off and on ever since I'd received the invitation to visit Martinique. I'd reread *Wide Sargasso Sea*, and of course it brought back memories of my meeting her as a child, when she'd lived near us in Cornwall. I'm sure my father had something going with her, though he's never hinted at it, and I've never asked him.

Yvette came back, looking cool from the pool, and we rowed over Kosovo; but it did no good. So, changing the subject, I said, 'I saw some beautiful butterflies.'

She rang Jean-Pierre, in Paris, and it was so gooey I would have puked if I hadn't taken myself off to the bar.

8

M Y MOOD was not much improved when, on another chokingly hot, humid morning, we caught the ferry across to Fort de France, then strolled through the narrow streets of shuttered shops and banks already familiar to me, already tedious. We passed the statue of the Empress Josephine, born on the island. She had shown no concern that slavery persisted here when it was being abolished elsewhere, and it seemed fitting that some nocturnal black Robespierre had cleanly decapitated her statue a few years ago.

I was running short of cigarettes. I longed for a Tesco, a Sainsbury, even a corner shop, for fuck's sake. This universal holiday was taking liberation too far. I was starting to believe Martinique would never open. There was one little market stall selling old books, and I found one that I thought might appeal to my father. Otherwise there was *rien*. French indulgence allied to Caribbean indolence. My Dad would have said: String a few of the buggers up!

We reached the city's architectural pride and joy, La Bibliothèque Schoelcher. Schoelcher had been the man who freed the slaves (whatever that phrase means), and donated his book collection to found a library. His friend Pierre Henri Picq had created this building – I quote from the guidebook – '*de fer et de verre*' ... an edifice '*audacieux et novateur*'. It was gaudy and Gaudí. Its external walls were festooned with EU and French flags, just as the plush modern airport was; and there were giant banners welcoming the *femmes* of Europe to this festival of *écrivaines*. It seemed so bizarre that I was apparently still in Europe, and this tropical island didn't exist in its own right. I would come across a red, black and green flag, but only chalked on walls in odd corners of the island, accompanied by the word Matnik. But officially Matnik did not exist. The black islanders had been liberated by being absorbed, as a goose is liberated from its nature by being stuffed with food and turned into *foie gras*.

The few people on the streets, including those hovering around the library doors, looked listless, apathetic. 'You go on in,' I said to Yvette, 'I'll just have a last cigarette.'

I also needed a cooling beer. I eyed a bar across the road. Astonishingly – no doubt because of the special event at the Schoelcher – it seemed to be open. I walked across, and entered a fan-cooled bar. I was served with a beer, and lit up again. If I missed the opening speech, with its predictable *l'humanité, la justice, l'âme, l'esprit féminin, la conscience européenne*, all to the good.

A young, slim, brown-skinned man was going around the bar offering people leaflets, with little success. When he glided to my table and offered me one, I glanced at it. I saw it was something to do with a meeting to discover one's African roots. I accepted it and said, '*Vous voulez une bière?*' Surprised and pleased, he said *Oui, merci*, and sat down. Quickly establishing that I was English, he moved skilfully into that language. 'Juan,' he said (and some uncatchable surname), offering his hand.

'Charlotte.'

He was a teacher, he told me. I was also a teacher, I said. I wasn't exactly on holiday on the island; I required him to keep this confidence: I was here on behalf of the IRA, the Irish freedom fighters. They might have to promise to decommission their weapons, as a ruse to fool the Brits, and they'd made contact with Matnik freedom fighters. Some of the weapons could help them mount a terrorist campaign against France, until such time as the armaments could be returned to Ireland. It was a sensitive mission, I said. Juan looked dismayed; didn't approve of violence, he said; and hadn't realised the Martinique independence movement was serious. He himself believed the island should be more independent, but didn't think it could go all the way. The islanders were too lazy and too spoiled.

Over a second and a third beer I confessed the real – well, the *ostensible* – purpose of my visit, and he was reassured and intrigued.

I warmed to him as we talked. I could see he was shy and idealistic. He was also sad beneath his smiles, like others I had met on this island. It was because of the women, he said. 'The young women here don't want to get married. If an educated man, unless he's rich, is looking for a nice, educated girl – they just don't want to know.'

'Well, that's happening everywhere. Yet you have so much to offer. You're intelligent, good-looking ...'

He accepted the compliment with an embarrassed turn of his head. 'If they want a baby, the state will look after them.'

'They marry the state.'

He nodded. 'It's a real problem. Are you married?'

'Widowed.'

'I'm sorry.'

'It was a long time ago ... But I assume you can have sex easily enough? I imagine attitudes are pretty free and easy?'

'Yes, but I'm not looking for that. I want a wife, a family.'

His polo shirt was well-ironed; it looked like the work of an adoring mother, but when I asked him if he lived at home with his parents, he said no; he had never known his Cuban father, and his mother lived in Guyana. Since university in Bordeaux, he valued his independence. Though his salary was meagre, he rented a one-room flat. I imagined his neatness, the precious books and computer, the clothes ironed, fresh, hanging in the wardrobe. A single bed along one wall, clean sheets, but the faintly stale scent in the air that hangs around young men who don't have regular sex, a smell of solitary vice.

I was surprised to learn he was thirty, as he looked younger. Still, he must look upon me almost as an old woman. I couldn't quite tell if he was attracted to me; he spoke of 'nice girls', 'educated, cultured girls': girls, not women; not women nudging forty. Well, I wasn't particularly bothered.

He didn't much enjoy my smoking; the ash-tray filling with butts. 'It's a very bad habit, I agree, Juan. I blame a tutor of mine for giving me a taste for tobacco smoke. He was a professor from Belgium, who smoked cigars. When I wasn't in the classroom he would open my desk and fill it with his smoke. He knew I desired him; and that when I came back and opened my desk I would breathe in his presence and almost faint with longing. In fact, that's how I had my first orgasm.'

'That's a terrible story, Charlotte! He was sexually abusing you!'

'I guess so; but it was fun.' At least, I added, he hadn't fucked me with his cigar, like Clinton. Juan looked embarrassed again.

'I'm shocking you, Juan.'

'No, no … What are you going to do now? Are you going back to the library?'

'No. I should do, but I just can't. I'll take the ferry back to our hotel.'

'Have you seen St Pierre and Mont-Pelée?'

I shook my head. 'I've seen hardly anything.'

'It would be an honour for me to drive you there, Charlotte. I have my car nearby.'

'What about your leaflets?'

He shrugged. 'To be truthful, I'm really only hoping to meet a nice, educated, cultured girl.'

We lingered for the bill. I waved away his offer to pay. Silent, I listened to the black couple on the next table, near the door. They were obviously, from their English, their accents and their attire, well-off Afro-Americans; she in a white blouse, blue skirt, he in smart shorts, shades, baseball cap. At that moment a poor down-at-heel Martiniquain came in, approached them, holding out his hand. 'I'm sorry, I don't speak French,' said the Afro-American woman: '*je ne parle pas français*.' Turned to her husband saying, 'I guess he's hungry.' But they ignored him – it's not wise to encourage beggars, even for ex-slaves it's not wise to encourage beggars – and the man gave up and wandered out.

9

H IS RENAULT was stuffy, non-air conditioned; but as we raced up the northern coast road there was a warm, though welcome, breeze. Leaning my head out of the window, letting my long hair stream away, expressing pleasure in my closed eyes, I heard him say, '"Reason, I sacrifice you to the evening breeze." That's Aimé Césaire, our poet, in some way the father of our modern island. He's very old now.' A politician too, he said; who'd been largely responsible for the change from French colony to French *département* fifty years ago. Juan thought it was right for that era; but now, he was not so sure; probably the island, he repeated sadly, couldn't stand independence; it would be like freeing a canary to fend for itself.

We moved inland, and the breeze died. He interrupted a long silence to say, surprisingly, 'Did you know *your* father, Charlotte?'

'Oh yes, I know my father! He's an antiquarian bookseller, or used to be. He'll be eighty in September, and he's almost blind; but otherwise pretty fit.' His loneliness, though, his sadness …

'And your mother?'

'She died a long time ago.'

'So you've lost her and your husband. That's sad. How did your husband die?'

'A heart attack.'

'Well … sudden, anyway; quite merciful.'

'Do you mind if I smoke, blowing it out the window? … He was

91

a designer, working on the Millennium Dome in London.' I had to explain the Dome to him. 'There's this gigantic human body in it, of doubtful sex, which people will be able to go inside and explore. David was working in the heart one day, when a jealous, crazed homosexual lover burst in and shot him.'

Juan, who had been nodding as I recounted my story, grimaced at its unexpected violent conclusion. He turned and saw my half-smile, which disconcerted him further. He risked a smile back. 'You like to joke, Charlotte!'

'Yes, I do.' Life was pretty unbearable, I explained, and I liked to escape from it sometimes. 'My husband's alive; but dead – you know?'

'I think so. But is he gay?'

'No.'

'We hate gays on this island. I'm sorry, I hate them too. I know we should like them, but we don't.' There was just one night club in Fort de France where they hung out. I asked him why there was hatred of gays. 'Because we have lost so much,' he said; 'we've lost our nationality, and our status as head of a family – the women don't need us; they don't care about paternity so long as the father is as white as possible. So you see, all we have left is our *machismo*. Gays threaten that ... Mont-Pelée,' he said, pointing ahead; and I saw the serene mountain-top that hid a fiery furnace.

He had turned off the coast road and we were climbing, into more and more lushness and rankness, a flamboyance of reds and greens, yellows and purples. He pointed out some trees whose foliage was spread out wide, like a Victorian lady's fan. 'Voyager trees,' he said. A little further: 'Anthuriums' ... Huge waxy-red flowers, with giant stamens. 'Besides, he said, 'I don't like what they do.'

'Fucking up the arse?'

He reacted with a slight jerk of his shoulder. 'Well … yes!' He kept his gaze straight, concentrating on the winding, rising lane.

I thought of adding to his discomfort by saying, 'I quite like it myself,' or 'Haven't you ever taken a girl up the arse?' but we were entering the plantation Macintosh, and its natural splendour made me swallow my words. 'I thought we could have a drink here,' he said.

'It's beautiful.'

There was no plantation house any more; no more Macintosh; (Juan didn't know anything about him); no more slaves, except one solemn guy at the ticket desk and a woman in the pretty, pagoda-shaped snack bar, and Juan, and I. All in our different ways. Just gigantic trees and bracken and anthuriums, and silence, and birdsong. Juan was pleased I was so enchanted.

While we sat in the pagoda a real tropical storm suddenly blew up, slanting rain lashed down outside, stirring every leaf, silencing the birds; the grass drummed, but then as quickly the rain softened to a patter, the birds reawakened, and then the rain heavier again, like tears welling and fading and welling up … and then tranquillity, the sun bathing the foliage.

It made me feel sad. My mother, so full of life and colour one moment, then the sudden storm of tears and desperation. And there was nothing my father could do. Nowadays they might have controlled it with lithium.

There was a tiny museum at the entrance/exit. An engraving showed naked Caribs, whom we Euros had expunged, dancing around a big pot.

The Renault took us down into St Pierre, the former elegant capital, 'Paris of the Caribbean', that the volcanic mountain had expunged in 1902. It was now just another sleepy little town, still with some ruined walls and the shell of a once-great opera house. I tried to imagine that shell filled with ladies in long white dresses, gentlemen in top hats and tails, and some splendid *Carmen* or *La Bohème* on the stage. The mountain had buried all thirty thousand inhabitants in a couple of minutes: all but the town's drunk, who survived because he was in an underground police cell. Vice rewarded. He spent the rest of his life exhibiting his burns in Barnum & Bailey's Circus.

The museum was full of old pictures and relics of the earthquake: trumpets and glasses, warped and melted. But the most potent symbol of mortality was in the box office, where an incredibly black beauty – long hair, wide smile, and huge intelligent eyes – was talking to a frail, toothless old lady, her shoulders as narrow as one of Lowry's stick figures, draped incongruously in a kind of white christening robe. When she heard me asking for tickets she beamed at me and started gabbling in English. She was St Lucian; thirty years ago had married a man from Martinique, but she still felt English. She had a nephew in Brixton, London. This was her daughter, she said proudly; and the incredible beauty smiled her huge flashing-white smile.

My tourist map showed a spot marked *tombeau des caraïbes* on the coast road north. I asked Juan what it was. He said it was where the last surviving Carib chiefs jumped off the cliff to their death, after drinking poison, rather than be killed by the white men. 'And as they leapt into the sea, they called on the sacred mountain to avenge them.'

I could see it in my mind. It moved me. 'Can we go there?'

'Of course; though there's nothing to see.'

Columbus. Cortez. NATO. Bastards.

In the dense, steamy heat of mid-afternoon, we snaked around the coast. He drew up at a dusty, barren spot where the sea was invisible on our left; and on our right, a great gouged-out grey expanse of quarry, stretching as far as one could see up the mountain side. We got out. On the seaward side was the first clear

94

evidence I'd seen of a people's anger. Painted in red along a concrete wall were the words: Génocide Amérindien, TRAITE et ESCLAVAGE des NOIRS: CRIMES EUROPEENS CONTRE L'HUMANITE. Then, after a carefully-drawn flag, a Creole phrase meaning Liberty for Matnik.

Juan, at my side, shook his head sadly. 'They're just a small number.'

'But thank God there are some!'

Across from the graffiti was a small bus shelter, and near it a stone bearing a tiny chalk message and an arrow, pointing away up the quarry: *tombeau*. I was confused; how could they have jumped from the cliff into the sea when the sign indicated the mountain? Juan couldn't explain. Maybe they jumped into a ravine, he said. He tried to dissuade me from going in search of it, but I had scrambled over the low hedge into the quarry dust, and set off, baking, up the side of a moon-crater. There had at least to be a memorial? This was important, this was a momentous place: the dying-place of the Caribs on Martinique. I struggled on and up, my clothes sticking to me, following excavator tracks, expecting at every turn to find some simple, dignified monument. Juan came after me, crying, '*Il n'y a rien!*'

I gave up; turned back with him.

'Don't feel too sorry for them,' he said, as we got back into the car; 'remember they exterminated the Arawaks, who were gentle farming people from the mouth of the Amazon. And probably ate them too!'

I felt he was sensitive in not speaking for a few miles of the southward journey. Carib after Carib leapt into the ravine, or the sea. As we joined a snail of traffic at St Pierre, he said, 'And the mountain did avenge them.'

'Yes. *Bien!*'

On the way back we stopped only once, at a roadside stall, to drink about a gallon of guava juice. Juan refused to drop me off at the ferry station in Fort de France, insisting on taking me all the way round the bay. Soon I regretted his kindness, for all at once the island – near the airport anyway – was like London at rush-hour; a total jam of cars and lorries. 'End of the holiday,' he said. This was what it was usually like; Martinique had more cars for its population than almost anywhere in the world, he said. For half an hour we didn't move: stuck near a sign that said *Speeding kills on Martinique.* Edging forward we came to *67 dead in 1998.* A little further and – *Are you in a hurry to die?* Everywhere honking, and mad drivers bumping up over traffic islands to go the other way, or speeding down bicycle lanes. At long last we were through the worst. I saw a pale, bony cow in a ditch; and remembered I had seen it before, sitting there impassive, on our coach-ride from the airport. Dusk was falling.

The hotel's guard, recognising me, lifted the barrier to let us into the grounds. I thanked Juan profusely for a wonderful day. 'I'd like to see you again, Charlotte,' he said.

'That would be nice. Ring me sometime. By the way, my name isn't Charlotte it's Miranda, Miranda Stevenson. I'm in room one-six-seven.'

He considered for a few moments; smiled at me. 'I like it just as much.' I laughed and leaned over to kiss him on the cheek.

Dusk was beginning to fall. I walked into reception just as a party of smart Air France crew members walked in. I pushed through quickly and said to the female receptionist, 'One-six-seven?' – the query in my voice because Yvette could have picked up the key. The girl's fixed smile faded and she moved aside to speak quietly to her male companion, who nodded. She came back to me with the key. Her face looked concerned. 'There have been many phone calls for you; you should call home immediately.' My knees went weak and I felt my heart hammer dementedly. I whispered a *merci* and moved away in a dream. The two hundred yard walk to our building seemed like a marathon; I couldn't lift my feet; I was nauseous. Something terrible had happened. Alison? Jeremy? My father? That would be better than my children, and perhaps most likely, because he was old; but still – unbearable. David? ... It would be a relief, by comparison with the others, but Ali and Jerry would be devastated, and so it would be dreadful too.

I couldn't fumble the key into the lock for a long time. At last I was in, into the cool, into the heartbreak. I hovered over the phone. It rang, screamed at me rather, just as I was about to lift the receiver. I grabbed it up. It was a smooth, masculine French voice, asking for Yvette, and I said for fucksake get off the line you stupid cuntstruck prick! but it came out in French as *'Elle n'est pas ici, Jean-Pierre.'* The voice, which no longer sounded so smooth, said, 'It's not Jean-Pierre, this is Alain, his brother. Jean-Pierre has had a car-crash; a bad one; he's in a coma on a life-support machine ...'

'Oh, shit!'

But suddenly all that huge weight had lifted from me; my heart was flying and singing like the bright birds at Macintosh. It wasn't one of mine! Alain was asking me if I would tell Yvette, and have her ring him. He gave me a number which I scribbled down.

When he had rung off, I threw myself on the bed. I was sorry for Yvette, but utterly joyous.

My heart gradually settled. I wanted to ring my kids, and my father, but it was midnight there – too late.

Desperate for a stiff drink and a swim, I changed and – after writing a note, FIND ME AT THE POOL – left the french windows slightly ajar. There was a spring in my step now, though I worried about having to tell her. I had a rum cocktail – a *planteur* – a lovely swim, and another *planteur*. I thought how strange death was: it could practically destroy you – as I'd known once, with my mother, oh my God yes – or you can be very sorry but it doesn't really touch you, you can enjoy a swim and a cocktail all the same. There was even a bit of *schadenfreude*, that thinks, You threw over a perfectly decent Welsh husband – I'd met him briefly, and he'd seemed perfectly okay, as husbands go – for a French smoothie, and this is what you get for it. Maybe a drooling quadriplegic.

I was out of our room less than half an hour, and she still wasn't back. I showered, then lay on the bed reading.

The door opened; Yvette looked tired and sweaty, but happy. 'What ever happened to you?' she exclaimed.

'I developed a bad headache.'

'I'm sorry. You missed a great day! I think my paper went down quite well, but you should have heard Alessandra Bellini – she was really wonderful!'

I rose from the bed, took hold of her hands. 'Yvette, sit down.' She did so, wondering, paling. 'I'm so sorry, my dear ...' She became demented, scurrying around the room like a headless chicken. I gave her water. I dialled the Paris number for her, and handed her the phone when Alain answered; went out onto the terrace, so as not to overhear her, and lit a cigarette. I had only one packet of Silk Cuts left; tomorrow at least Martinique would be open.

She burst out through the doors, wild-eyed and sobbing, looking like Clytemnestra.

I was efficient: rang Air France, establishing they could get her on the last flight out tonight, if she hurried; did most of her packing for her; sorted out clean jeans, T-shirt and underwear for her; got reception to order a taxi; went with her to wait for it; hugged her a lot; kissed her goodbye, telling her she must not give up hope; waved her off.

I didn't feel excessive sympathy for her. She'd only known him a couple of years. *She* didn't know what it was like to be called to the headmistress's study – to be hugged by her father and told her mother was dead. At a lively restaurant along the marina, I flirted with an energetic waiter, and observed the tables where brittle middle-aged French tourists – French French – in micro-skirts and too much make-up gazed hungrily at their young coloured gigolos. I felt serene, still savouring my escape from unbearable grief. The gigolos let their gazes stray towards me on occasion. My long black hair and my grey-green eyes can still attract looks, even if my tits have started to sag a bit.

I found myself humming an Annie Lennox song on the way back. There was relief, also, in having the room to myself, and to be rid of the strain of Yvette's company. We'd been friendly enough as teaching colleagues, a decade since, but we'd exhausted those memories in the Business Class of the Air France flight.

10

THE PHONE ROUSED ME at about seven. It was David, calling me from the Dome. 'I was worried about you, darling; you said you'd ring in a couple of days.'

'I was planning to yesterday, but ...' I explained what had happened, and he said, 'How awful' and 'Poor woman.'

'I was out of my mind thinking something had happened to the kids, or you, or Dad. Are the kids okay?'

'They're fine.'

I asked him how work was going and he said, pissing awful, he had to come up with ideas for what to put in the Faith Zone. No one wanted it at all, except the Church. There would be endless opportunity for causing offence to people. David said, with a black chuckle, he thought they should just have giant TV screens showing the Christian Serbs killing innocent Moslem Albanians.

He knows we don't see eye-to-eye about Kosovo, and very swiftly our conversation becomes another argument. He's all for going in with land forces and knocking the shit out of the Serbs: which is strange for a left-wing pacifist; but then, this recurrent row, and our disagreement over the Euro, is really a mask for a more profound rift; and we switched back to what I was doing, the kids' homework, and so on, before closing it down. I called my father, but got Alice, the village woman who 'does' for him. He was out for his constitutional. I had a chat with Alice, whom I'd known since my teens. It was pleasant to hear her friendly Cornish tones for a couple of minutes.

Then, just as I was stepping out of the shower, another trill of the phone. This time, Juan. 'I finish school early, Miranda. I'd like to show you the Diamond Rock.'

'That would be lovely,' I said. 'I'll leave early too – shall we meet in that bar? Say, at two?'

I took the ferry across. Fort de France was now humming. I bought a carton of Marlboro Light, and a nice red skirt. At the Schoelcher Library I almost died of boredom for three hours, listening to pretentious lectures – knowing mine would be equally so; but at least I familiarised myself with the set-up. Everyone I spoke to looked sad about Yvette, though of course none of them could give a shit.

In the heavenly, smoky, sordid freedom of the bar, Juan was waiting. He ordered me a beer. The only problem – we couldn't hear ourselves speak; a monstrous TV screen, turned to full volume, gave us the *pock-pock-pock*, with hysterical commentary and crowd shrieks, of the French Lawn Tennis Championships. We left almost at once; found his car, and headed south out of the city, climbing up past the substantial houses of the *beki*, the native whites who – so Juan said – still owned most of the island. Then to the motorway, round the bay and the airport, where we'd been caught in a traffic jam – and were snarled up again. '*La vitesse tue* …' I told him about my room-mate's tragedy.

I was beginning to hate this part of the island. Not only was the traffic dense, but on each side was an industrial wasteland – it might have been Wolverhampton. It was a relief when we were through, and on narrow, quieter roads towards Les Anses and Diamant. I saw again the pale, skeletal cow, lying in a roadside ditch. I wondered what she made of it all.

Diamant proved to be a small, quiet hamlet by the sea. For-

101

merly, Juan told me, it had been a bustling slave-port. The slaves, as they emerged in their chains from the hellish voyage, were referred to as Congos, from the place in Africa that had bred them.

He showed me the Diamond Rock, offshore. Cut into many facets, it did seem to glitter like a diamond. He related its occupation by the English during the Napoleonic Wars, and I pretended I hadn't read it in the guidebook.

The surf is restless, angry, white-crested here, because it's the Atlantic; and it strikes me that there is no land between here and Land's End in Cornwall, where I grew up. It's a kind of close connection, and at the same time far distant, like sex.

Too wild to swim here. We drove along the coast. I wanted the beach where I'd encountered Jerry. It already seemed an age ago. We came to it; Jerry was there serving, or rather lounging: his face lighting up when he saw me, falling when he saw the smart-looking guy following quickly behind.

Postcards …

25 - 5 - 99

Dearest Dad,

This rock really does glitter like a diamond. It was taken by Lieutenant Hood (later Admiral) two hundred years ago, and held for three years against the French. By an incredible system of ropes and pulleys he constructed a fortress – complete even with a hospital – on the summit! Rule Britannia, what! I hope you're not feeling quite so low. I'll be seeing you soon. I'm looking for voodoo, but there's none; it's just French girocheques.

Lots of love, Miranda xxx

Dearest Jeremy,

This mountain is still an active volcano. The last time it erupted, in 1902, it destroyed all of the capital, St Pierre, killing 30,000 people. Only one guy, the town drunk, survived. I'll be back, I'm sure, before you get this card, but hope you are helping Daddy and not monopolising the TV and video! How's the revision going? Remember, Westminster's a *bloody* good school, so don't take the Entrance too lightly.

Longing to see you,

Love, Mummy xxx

Dearest Ali,

This is a most beautiful old plantation – no house left but wonderful garden, as you can see. Saw a hummingbird flitting over bananas – magical sight! Another highlight was a butterfly house. It's very steamy weather; I'm baking on a beach. I should be at the conference but I've played hookey for an afternoon!

Longing to see you,

Love, Mummy xxx

Darling,

I've driven to this beach, which is quiet and beautiful, this afternoon, when I should be at the conference. But I've been working quite hard, and Yvette's news was very upsetting, naturally, so thought I deserved a break. Am drinking a *planteur* (rum cocktail) and chatting to a Martinique teacher. She tells me the schools here are excellent – that's the French welfare state for you!

Longing to see you, Mandy xxx

Theo,

Sprawled out on this beach – as serene and gorgeous as it looks – being fought over (mildly) by two Martiniquains! Black big-dicked Jerry, a beach boy/bartender, was crestfallen when I turned up with shy, educated Juan – who's crestfallen because he senses an intimacy! Just light flirtations, – it's much too hot to screw, even if I were inclined to. So don't worry that I'm going off the rails. See you next week, if Jerry or Juan haven't carried me off! Doing my CB tomorrow.

Love, Mandy

It had been a nice afternoon. I did think of Yvette, rushing straight from the flight to see her partner in hospital, and I felt sorry for her; but at the same time the awareness of her pain increased my own wellbeing. Fate had nasty things in store for me too, but – thank God – not yet. Juan was his courteous, bashful self – keeping his eyes averted when I swam topless – and Jerry was pleasingly resentful of him. I could easily have avoided this beach – there were so many. I had to admit to myself I enjoyed the competition.

We drove back to Trois Ilets as the sun dipped. I invited him, naturally, to have dinner with me. Throughout our Creole meal he remained charming, a little flirtatious, but far too polite – or uncertain of himself – to make a pass. It was left to me: putting my hand on his and suggesting he might like to come back with me. Dropping his gaze – he'd love to, he said, but I was married.

'In name only. My husband has a mistress …' (I had no idea if this was true; it seemed unlikely.) 'I like you very much, Juan, and you attract me very much …' – stroking his hand. 'Please come.'

He was flustered. 'I like you too.' I could see desire and decorum fighting in his anguished face, like the English and the French over the Antilles. 'I'd love to come, but – as I said to you, Miranda – I don't really like casual sex.'

That did him credit, I responded; but life was short: look what had happened to Yvette's boyfriend: healthy, rich, young – and now brain-dead. Anyway, I added – echoing many a male chat-up line I'd heard – we needn't have sex; we could just lie together; it would just be lovely to hold him and be held.

He was still considering, or appearing to be, while we walked from the marina to the hotel. As we reached his car, and I drew him to me, he murmured, 'Yes, let's go to your room.'

We lay, naked, just hugging for a while, and kissing. He seemed to have a boy's awkward kiss. I started to stroke him, but his cock, smaller than Jerry's or even David's, remained fairly limp. The conviction grew in me that he had had very few girls; as indeed I should have guessed from his sadness, his non-acceptance of Caribbean promiscuity, his hungering for a 'nice, educated, cultured girl' who wanted marriage. Possibly also, I had to admit, he might find me too old for him. His touches were clumsy, he scarcely knew where to put his fingers.

Noticing the bite-marks on my breast and neck, he asked how they had come about. I said, 'My husband can be quite sadistic.' He did not quite say 'The brute!' but his expression conveyed it.

When I gently caressed his perineum and his arsehole – and slid a finger up – he grew suddenly erect. It hardly ever fails. Drawing back, he said, 'You're sure?' and I nodded.

He asked me if I had condoms. I did; but did not want to use them, so I said no. Then we can't make love, he said; one had to be very careful about SIDA. 'I know I am clean, but *you* can't know that, and you mustn't take the risk.' I said I was willing to, I trusted him, and he could trust me. I wasn't promiscuous, and nor was my husband.

'But you said he has a mistress.'

'Well, I don't know that for sure; he probably hasn't. If he has, I'm sure she's some nice middle-class Englishwoman. But okay, I give up, I do have some.'

I went to a drawer, fumbled in it, and handed him the packet. 'I want you to know I don't make a habit of this,' I said, truthfully. David had given me some crotchless knickers one Valentine's Day; they had a little pocket containing the condoms. I've never worn the knickers, but in packing hurriedly I'd thrown them in my case with other underwear, not realising. Theo, my analyst, would have a chuckle over that.

By the time he'd opened the packet and stroked the condom on, he was understandably not ready again. And I was quite dry too. I stroked and penetrated him with one hand, and stroked myself with the other; and at last we were both more-or-less ready. He slid in, uncertainly, half-limply. 'I'm sorry,' he whispered, 'it's been too long since I did this.'

'Don't worry; and people have to get to know each other. The first time is bound to be awkward.'

But after he'd spent into the condom and collapsed on me, he murmured, 'It was beautiful, Miranda!'

'Yes, it was.' I stroked his hair absently.

It hadn't been beautiful; but in a way it had. As one may find a production of an opera by enthusiastic amateurs more enjoyable than one that's professional but routine. He padded to the bathroom; I leaned down beside my bed to click off my little recorder, then I fingered another button to bring myself off.

Returning from his shower, he slipped on his shorts and shirt and sat down by the TV, looking uncomfortable. 'That was great!' he repeated. He picked up one of the two exercise books I'd put down on top of the TV. 'Humphry Davy,' he read; 'I've seen that name somewhere.'

'He was a famous English chemist. Invented the miners' safety lamp. He came from where I grew up – Penzance, in Cornwall, in the west of England – and gave his name to the grammar school I attended. Those notebooks are twenty years old – I stole several when I left school!'

Flicking through the first of them he observed, 'What wonderful penmanship! It looks as if you were practising it.'

'I was. I had three months' holiday before going on to university, and nothing much to do. I decided to do something special for my father's sixtieth birthday. He collected Victoriana. I rewrote the ending of one of his favourite novels – a dozen or so pages – then laboriously copied it onto special old paper I found in a drawer. Of course, looking at it now, it was very juvenile writing, but I was quite proud of it at the time.'

'What a lovely present, Miranda! Your father must have been so pleased.'

'I guess so.'

He looked wistful. I remembered he'd never known his father, or even who he was. I moved off the bed, into a sitting position. 'Well, if you'll excuse me, I have some preparing to do.'

'Of course' – reaching for his sandals and slipping them on. He came to give me a sweet, shy, farewell kiss; the kiss of an awkward teenage boy; the kiss Jeremy will offer some girl in a year or two. It tingled on my lips for a few seconds, like the brush of a butterfly-wing, after he'd left.

I sat in the bar, with a *planteur*, the second notebook open, and thought about that long-ago summer. Except it was no summer, it rained most of the time. And I'd raged. He'd promised to take me to France, for a camping holiday, just the two of us, before I left for the big world – or at least that portion of it represented by Manchester University. Instead, he'd got himself involved with a pretentious art historian from New York, visiting Cornwall to research the Newlyn School. I was mad at him for cancelling our holiday, and I was jealous – oh, indeed I was, dear reader! I hated her. For five years it had been just he and I, in the rambling book-filled house overlooking the Atlantic, in the midst of the moor. Oh, there were women; I knew he was screwing the local woman, who 'did' for him in more ways than one; that was fine, Alice knew her place, was just glad that at forty, an 'old maid', she was screwing her cultured employer. But this Judith, this Brooklyn Jewish harridan – she was clearly out to get him, and he'd fallen; they'd planned to marry. I felt she was a real Judith, out to cut off his head.

Twenty years on, I could still feel my emotions of that time, had to blink away tears at the hurt of the cancelled holiday.

Yet I'd created for him that special birthday gift, trying to follow the style of Charlotte's own careful hand. My father was forever buying up the contents of old libraries, stowing unwanted items into ancient bureaux and cupboards and forgetting them. Rummaging one rainy boring day, I'd come across some quill pens and a dozen or so sheets of yellowing manuscript paper – more than a century old, to judge by cuttings from the *West Briton* I found in the same corner of the same long-unopened drawer.

The pens, the paper, had germinated my idea. I felt, now, *moved* by that young girl's generosity and love.

'Another *planteur*, Madame Charlotte?' Dabbing my eyes with a tissue, I looked up. The friendly, forward waiter. I pretended to have to blow my nose.

'Yes, why not?'

Of course I'd told my excited father the manuscript was real; said I'd answered an ad in some obscure journal; showed him the letter I'd typed on a friend's ancient machine, thanking me in fairly illiterate language for the receipt of my hundred pounds, swearing me again to absolute confidentiality – implying that she wasn't necessarily the owner of the goods sold, hence the ridiculously low price. Another holidaying school-friend had sent this letter to me from Ireland, the address simply 'Dublin' ... Told him I'd used money inherited from Mum. I wanted him to be fooled, or at least uncertain, only for a day or two – or even an hour! Long enough for him then to say how brilliantly I'd done it and what a clever girl I was ... Hilarious really; it shouldn't have fooled him for a moment. But there's no one so blind as someone with an obsession. He wanted to believe it authentic; and all I could do was to help Charlotte's message along – which was that you should beware of rushing into marriage, when you hadn't exorcised the powerful manic depressive wife who'd thrown herself off a cliff ...

Well, essentially. Reading between the lines.

Because he obviously *hadn't* exorcised her, and still hasn't. And really there was only one woman who could bring her back, assuage his longing a little, by stepping at times literally into her shoes. Black high heels, or the red courts I wore to the Sixth Form Christmas Dance.

Well, for whatever reason, he eventually gave his Jewish art historian the boot. By then I'd gone to university, got into sex and drugs, failed my first year exams, had my first breakdown, then went to a third-rate poly where I scraped a pass (almost impossible not to) and met David, Art and Design Tutor with Wife and Toddler.

'Thank you.'

'You're welcome.' He's probably learnt this phrase from handling Canadians from the pussy-flights.

Then, marriage, kids, Valium, a flat in Sidcup, a maisonette in Blackheath, a lectureship in Women's Studies in the same third-rate poly, now laughingly described as a university, a minor reputation as a narrowly-based academic, Prozac, an increasing urge to escape from reality into fiction, as that eighteen-year-old gym-slipped girl did. There you have it, dear reader.

Well now, Jane ... I opened my notebook. Do we want stuff about the voyage? No, I don't think so, this isn't Captain Hornblower ...

11

ON DISEMBARKING in the bustling port of St Pierre, Martinique, we were at once bombarded by colour, noise, smell and vitality. I felt dizzy and unstable from the novelty and intensity of tropical life, in addition to the unsteadiness which arose from suddenly being on firm ground. Having become accustomed to being tossed on the ocean, we experienced *terra firma* as a constant flux. The more remarkable it was, therefore, to see so many female Negro slaves, in colourful costume, and barefoot, walking at high speed – indeed sometimes running, with baskets of fruit and vegetables balanced on their heads; and some carried pitchers of water in that way and while we watched them they never spilled a drop.

'We' embraced a third person now: a short, stocky French sailor. Grace had spent an eventful voyage being warmly courted by this mariner, M. Maillard. He was due to retire from the service following the return journey, and told Grace he would be quite happy to settle, if she wished it, in some southern English port, such as Margate. He bore no ill will against the former enemy, though he had taken part in the great Battle of Trafalgar. Grace was drawn to him, in her quiet, unemotional way; asked for my opinion, I urged acceptance, and they were duly married by the ship's captain. Her spouse seemed agreeable enough; quite content to allow Grace to remain here for a few weeks with me, as she wished; and proved to be exceedingly helpful to us in our sudden transposition to a strange island.

The city of St Pierre had a most attractive appearance. It had been, as it were, carved out of the side of a mountain, which we were informed was volcanic, but which mercifully had not erupted in recent times. We observed a profusion of buildings, few higher than two storeys, mostly painted yellow and with attractive red-tiled roofs, spread out on the mountain slopes. Not for nothing was St Pierre known as the Paris of the Antilles.

We were met by a polite, elderly Frenchman in a white suit and panama hat, M. Trémond, a friend of Mr Mason, who had arranged for him to greet us and help us with lodging and travel arrangements. He escorted us to a quiet lodging away from the noisy taverns where mariners were wont, he said, to enjoy themselves excessively after a long period at sea. Nor did I imagine that they were without female company – there seemed to be a greater proportion of females than of males in the streets.

After we had settled into respectable, clean rooms, M. Trémond showed us more of the town. We saw the splendid opera house and cathedral – of the Roman Catholic faith. Nevertheless, I went inside for a few minutes to offer my thanks for a safe voyage and to pray for help in finding Edward's son. Walking through the narrow busy streets, I could not help remarking on the vivacity of many of the Negroes, even though (unlike in our English colonies) they were still slaves. They bore themselves proudly and it appeared, happily enough, even when engaged in menial and laborious activities. I have seen free English labourers appear much more sullen and discontented.

M. Trémond observed that the slaves were generally well-treated, provided that they were obedient, and that there was not in the French colonies, as there used to be in the English, the detestable practice of splitting up slave families.

The delightful bay, which one kept seeing through the gaps in the buildings, was full of ships from all parts of the globe. It was a most charming spectacle.

We remained two days and nights in St Pierre, resting and getting our land-legs. Then it was time to board another vessel, which would transport us further to the south of the island. Grace took leave of her husband, who would shortly be making the long return voyage. I felt sorry to be the cause of their parting, but both assured me that they did not object, since they hoped to have a long life together, and Grace was as eager as I to try to find Bertha Mason's son.

I had already made enquiries in the town, but no Robert Rochester was known. It might well be of course that this voyage of mine would prove sterile – perhaps he had moved away to another island, or indeed to England in search of people of his own race and culture; though Mr Mason had told me he believed him to be still in Martinique. I could only hope, and try.

Bidding farewell to M. Trémond, our kind helper, we set sail again, on a vessel taking cargo to Fort Royal. There were only six passengers. Late in the voyage we learned that there were two or three dozen slaves below deck. I was assured they had been provided with ample water; yet I felt uncomfortable to have been walking about on deck above their heads.

Fort Royal proved to be a small port in poor condition: many buildings had been badly damaged by a recent earthquake. We spent only one night there, then hired a coach to take us to the port of Diamant, which I had been informed was close to the plantation Mason. We found the port to be a sizeable town, almost as busy and bustling as St Pierre. A large vessel, one of many in the harbour, was disgorging its slaves. These, in their irons, had none of the vivacity of slaves in the capital, but bore all the hallmarks of recent captivity and a dreadful voyage. Despair and exhaustion

113

were written on their faces. Had I ever doubted the arguments of Mr Wilberforce, I should have doubted no longer.

The *auberge* which M. Trémond had recommended to us was in the charge, that day, of a greasy-looking and inebriated man. I did not care much for the way he looked at me, and resolved to spend as little time as possible in his company. He pointed out to us a large, craggy, picturesque rock, out to sea, which he said my countrymen had occupied for a considerable time during the tumultuous wars. I could, I thought, make out evidence of human occupation, at the very summit of the rock, and I marvelled at the audacity and ingenuity of our navy in being able to overcome the opposition of nature and the French. I confess that I felt a warm patriotism steal over me at that moment.

On being informed that the plantation was not far distant, I decided that we would go there on foot. We waited for the day to cool a little before setting off, following a track up a hill. We entered into a veritable jungle of tall, dense trees and gigantic, luxuriously-coloured plants. It was beautiful in its lush, wild way. Grace was fearful of snakes and insects, and we were aware that our unprotected faces were being sharply bitten. Our pace slackened as the merciless heat burned down on us.

At last we reached the outskirts of our goal. A host of slaves cutting cane in the fields looked at us curiously. We arrived at the house, a white wooden building with a cool-looking veranda entirely running round it. We were greeted – coolly indeed – by the present owner, a Frenchman. The plantation had passed out of the Mason family. M. Lamont, grey-haired, burnt almost as black as the Negroes by the sun, and somewhat ungracious, listened to my halting explanation impatiently, then told me he had no knowledge whatever, either of an Edward Rochester or a Robert Rochester. He had written to M. Trémond telling him so; our journey was a wasted one.

During this one-sided conversation, Grace was looking uncomfortable – unwell – and kept fanning herself, even though the veranda where we sat was cool. Suddenly she collapsed in a faint. Our surly host, at last showing some hint of humanity, instructed two house-servants to assist her into the house. They laid her on a chaise-longue. Her eyes opening, she murmured to me, 'Sorry, miss – feel dreadful.' I asked the master if there were a bedroom where she could rest awhile, and he assented. Two black girls helped her upstairs, followed by me.

By nightfall Grace was worse; she had vomited many times, and was tossing feverishly on the bed. Clearly it would be impossible for us to return to Diamant. M. Lamont grudgingly offered me a room; but Grace was in such a bad way that I stayed up all night with her, fanning her and bathing her forehead, dozing only fitfully from time to time.

The next day she was no better; I begged the master to send for a doctor; but he seemed not to hear me. Two of the house-slaves were kind, especially the older of the two, called Emilie, a woman of generous girth. They bought me unfamiliar but refreshing fruit, and insisted that I rest at times while they took my place at the bedside. Emilie's Creole French was at the very edge of my understanding; but I was able to talk to her a little, to the extent that she understood I had come searching for a young white man, who had once lived there. She said there were old folk on the plantation who might know something, and I should talk to them in their huts.

I gathered she told fortunes by reading the palm, and I asked her if she would read mine. She took my small white hand in her plumply creased black hand and gazed deeply and solemnly at my palm. I believe that her message was this: that I would face a choice, of a long life without love or a short life with much love. I told her I would gladly accept the second, but felt I was much more likely to be awarded the first. I do not think she understood me.

I asked her if Grace would recover. Entering the sickroom, where my companion was drowsing, Emilie took her sweaty hand, palm up. After examining it for a few moments, she said there was nothing to worry about. She would return across the seas to her homeland, but not for long – sailing back to this island, she would spend the rest of her life here, happily.

On the morning of the third day, Grace's fever reached a climax. Alone with her, I listened to her ravings. She spoke to her lost son – or to Bertha's lost son – sometimes saying 'Georgie' and sometimes 'Robert'. I think I heard her say, 'And then the little girl! Oh my poor little daughter!' She cried out, 'Edward! Edward!' several times, again seeming to see him in the room. Suddenly she ripped open the nightgown which had been found for her, exposing her full bosom; her legs and arms thrashed about, tearing away the sheet that had covered her; at the same time her face, which I was attempting in vain to bathe, took on a coarser, darker appearance – I cannot say how – but I was frightened to see a face that was more that of Bertha than Grace's. That fearsome face seemed at one moment lewd, at another full of hate; she spat at me, and hissed, 'You think I am *your* slave, Edward, but in truth you are mine!' I reeled back from her. She was moaning, grunting, crying out, her legs wantonly open and kicking at some unseen enemy or despoiler.

I could not bear any more of it, but rushed from the room – down the stairs – and out of the house. I stood leaning against a veranda support, panting.

But that hour marked a turning point in Grace's illness. Her fever cooled, and by dusk she was able to take some nourishment and talk to me, weakly but reasonably. Later that day, while she slept as peaceful as a child, I went with Emilie to visit some of the old slaves. I still felt shaken by what I had witnessed: by her use of my husband's Christian name; which suggested intimacy, even of a savage kind. She had told me he had never touched her; but should I ever have put my trust in a woman who had once been a common whore, no whit better than the whores plying their trade in St Pierre?

My mind spinning with these painful thoughts, I followed the fat Negress through a barrier of trees into a clearing: and was faced by an image of still greater horror. A young male slave, entirely naked, hung by his bound wrists from the branch of a tree; his head had slumped sideways onto his shoulder, his eyes were closed. He was twisting slowly. Bloody wounds scarred his muscular back. 'He tried to escape,' Emilie murmured to me. I felt for the first time, the reality of Golgotha.

12

'CHARLOTTE BRONTË was an extraordinary liar.'

I waited while, at the other microphone, a Frenchwoman de-claimed, '*Charlotte Brontë était une menteuse extraordinaire ...*' The repetition, especially in philosophical French, made the words sound almost true. I went on: 'A woman brought up in the narrow world of a vicarage, in a remote corner of northern England, in a taboo-ridden society, with a fairly remote father, and only two sisters and a brother for companionship, would inevitably be forced into a life of deceit, of feelings and thoughts withheld – even from her own self. In puberty especially, she would have believed that she alone had wicked thoughts and feelings; she alone, perhaps, in the whole world of decent, respectable – if not angelic – creatures. So began her lying, her pretence ...

'But as time went on she used it to great effect, by becoming a superb novelist. Not all novelists are liars; the further a novelist departs from reality as we experience it, the less of a liar he or she is. There is no way in which Danielle Steele and Stephen King lie; but Tolstoy does, and Proust; and so does Charlotte Brontë ...

'They lie, in the sense that their material and subject are their own lives, their own emotions. But they distort them, twist them, partly to make a fiction, partly because they themselves are half-unconscious of the personal realities that the launch of a *roman*, a romance, allows them to explore. Their novels therefore become more like poems – which have multiple visions and layers ...

'But who is this Charlotte Brontë? ...' (*'Qui est cette Charlotte Brontë? ...'*)

I saw a figure slip in from the murky rear of the library: Juan, in smart white shirt and tie, and dark trousers. He found a seat. I was pleased he had managed to get here, as he had said he would try to do. I moved into a potted history of Charlotte's life, concluding with: 'After so many years of intense loneliness, she married her father's dull-seeming curate, Mr Nicholls, whom she had derided to her friends for many years. They lived at Haworth, with her father – her first husband – in a veritable *ménage à trois*. She claimed to be happily married; but, after so many fictions, can we trust Charlotte? Maybe he surprised her with his passion. We don't know. Anyway, she enjoyed only nine months of happiness, reasonable contentment, or misery, before she died – of an uncertain illness.'

It wasn't an easy talk to pitch. Most of my audience, local people drawn in out of curiosity, would scarcely have heard of the Brontës, whereas a few, the mainland *intelligentsia*, had every major novel in every major language filed away and structurally analysed in their computer minds. I could almost see contempt on those faces as I launched into a summary of the plot of *Jane Eyre*. After that, I lost the locals when I spoke about different characters as aspects of Charlotte – Miss Temple, the patient, longsuffering goody-goody she was expected to be; Mr Rochester, the domineering, sexually experienced, cosmopolitan gentleman she would have loved to be; and Bertha Mason ('born perhaps on this very island'), the hysteria and madness produced by the impossible conflict. I paid graceful tribute to *Wide Sargasso Sea*, as a brilliant exploration of Bertha. Finally, I talked of Grace Poole, Bertha's jailer ... 'Grace kept Charlotte's unruly id closely-confined; she symbolises all that decorum and conventionality which cut off her breathing like a Victorian corset ...' (or like my mother's 1960-ish corselette, which I have not-breathed in at various times and rather enjoyed.) 'But Grace had the saving grace of getting drunk now and then; so allowing the "madwoman in the attic" to escape for a while – allowing Charlotte, more importantly, to slash men, rip up wedding apparel, and set fire to beds! It is in the tension of enforced restraint and wild bursting-out that Charlotte Brontë made her indelible mark ... Thank you.'

I inclined my head, sat down. There was uncertain clapping. I stood again. 'Before I take questions,' I said, 'I would like to express my gratitude to the organisers of "*L'Europe des Femmes Libérées*". I think it's wonderful that the European Union sponsors this event so lavishly, in a different country each year. I think it's great that France, whose turn it was this year, chose to hold it in one of its most remote provinces. It has not only allowed a great many academics, cultural advisors, and in many cases their partners, the opportunity to enjoy a very special island, but it will hopefully encourage its people to vote in the forthcoming European elections. After all, what would the slaves have given to be represented by an MEP, or part of an MEP, in Brussels? How life has improved for the Martiniquains! Of course, much remains to be done. The state could be far more generous to the unemployed and single mothers; but when I look at your fine roads, your innumerable cars, your television, and think, This is what Europe has done – to make up partially for its rapes – this is what it means to be European ... then I feel thankful and proud.'

I thought my exercise in irony might have gone over the top, but the clapping this time was whole-hearted. I smiled my gratitude, invited questions. Was Brontë a feminist? ('I guess so.') Did she have a European consciousness? ('I guess so.') Could I say a few words about where she lived? ('Well, Yorkshire was very remote from the intellectual and cultural centre, London. So she was provincial in being a woman and provincial geographically too, and this was very important, as I tried to say. I can understand it; I grew up near Land's End, in the far west: very close, as it happens, to where Charlotte's mother grew up.')

I saw Juan's hand raised and I pointed to him. An attendant held a mike in front of him. 'Dr Stevenson,' he said, 'you say you can understand her, and you obviously identify with her very strongly. Do you think, if she lived today, her life would be like yours?'

I smiled. 'That's an interesting question! Yes, I think she might have followed a similar track. She'd have read English, probably, gone to London, taken a Ph.D – which might have interfered with her creativity. She'd have married … I'm rather unusual in that I've only married once and I've stayed married … she might by now be on her second marriage, or be divorced and bringing up a couple of children on her own! Who can tell? She'd probably, like me, be teaching in a university. In other words, she'd be a much less interesting person!'

I smiled again and he smiled back, looking pleased with himself for asking a good question. I felt warm towards him; wanted that awkward, clumsy lovemaking again.

There were no more hands raised. I stepped down and made a rapid escape to the exit. I rejoiced in the air, and then the nicotine rush. Juan joined me outside. 'You were so good, Miranda. I'm glad I caught most of it – I had to rush from school.'

'Thank you for coming.'

'A drink?'

'I'd love to, but I'd better get back.' I said there was a dinner tonight, and he could come with me if he liked. He screwed up his face in disappointment – unfortunately there was a meeting of the Afro-Caribbean Society he couldn't possibly miss. And after – in answer to a further suggestion, for today I had come by car around the bay so wasn't bound by ferry-times – he simply had to mark exam papers. But tomorrow, after school? I said I was flying home in the evening, but I'd like to see him again – ring me in the morning. Wistfully he was riffling through my tattered *Jane Eyre*; I gave it to him, and said I'd send him a book of critical essays, *Eyre and Angels*, that I'd edited. He thanked me effusively; there were so few English books here. We kissed cheeks, said *au revoir* till tomorrow. I went back in to listen to Gretel Wildgans talk about Clara Viebig.

I dozed off during the Germanic angst, and my drowse continued and deepened as some Sorbonne woman discussed Suzanne Dracius-Pinalie, a Martinique novelist who, of course, was representing France. (Yvette, originally from Luxemburg, had presented a poet of that small nation.) Farewell speeches passed me by totally.

The celebration dinner was to be at a restaurant not far from headless Josephine. The day was by now a shade cooler, and the walk revived me.

One long table. I managed to get myself seated near two obvious dykes, Irmgard from Denmark, and Wanda from Holland, who had paired off during the conference (or maybe they knew each other before: who could tell?), and who seemed unpretentious. We exchanged greetings; they said they'd really liked my talk, and I said I'd unfortunately missed theirs as I'd had a migraine. The heat; ah yes, they could sympathise; it was almost unbearable. A long line of girls in traditional costumes filed in, looking down shyly, and several people on our table clapped. The girls went and seated themselves at a long second table. I gathered they were voluntary helpers.

I longed to be served with a drink. The waitresses moved very slowly and resentfully. For fuck's sake, I thought, they're supposed to be French! So why can't they stir themselves a bit? At last our *hors d'oeuvres* appeared, but still no wine.

Along the table the conversation was strained and stilted. It was post-feminist, second-stage dialectic – all this nodding and affirming and being understanding and respecting everyone's opinion. I had an almost overwhelming impulse to stretch out my arm and sweep all the glasses and cutlery within my reach onto the floor. I had another impulse to smash my fist into the face of the woman beside me, Maria Gonzales, with whom I was making polite small talk. These violent urges come over me sometimes, and I have not always resisted them; but I did on this occasion. At last some wine. I wanted to smoke between courses, but it was *verboten*. I made up for it by drinking; the dykes and I made sure we had half a dozen bottles in front of us. By the time the tropical fruit salad came, the dinner party was noisy and people were actually laughing. I told the lezzes about my Martinique friend who was homophobic and who said Martinique men in general were. I didn't know if it included lesbians. He'd mentioned one gay club. 'We've been there,' Irmgard said; 'it's not bad. The Papillon. We thought we'd go tonight. You want to come with us?'

'Why not?'

Finding that it was some distance away, and on my homeward route out of Fort de France, I offered to drive us. They wondered if I was in a fit state, but I pointed out this wasn't London or Amsterdam or Copenhagen, and I would drive carefully. Waiting for them outside the restaurant *toilette*, seeing passers-by through a haze, I found myself confronted by one of the traditionally-dressed volunteers, fabulously lovely, a Sheba. Glittering with flamboyant earrings and necklaces, the girl touched my arm and begged my forgiveness: she'd been so overwhelmed by the situation, asked to greet and take care of one of the distinguished scholars; but how stupid of her to have looked down the wrong column and addressed me as Madame Brontë ... 'I am glad you did not need me,' she said, looking anything but glad, looking indeed close to tears; 'though I would have liked to talk to you; I am a student of literature and philosophy.'

Dimly, now, I saw the plain, bespectacled girl in a neat cotton frock who had greeted me at the airport. I slurred, gazing at her face, 'O, she doth hang upon the cheek of night, Like a rich jewel in an Ethiop's ear!'

'*Comment?*'

'You look so beautiful! If I were a man I would fall in love with you.'

'*Oh, merci!*'

Shyly she presented her conference programme and asked me if I would sign it. I did so. As she wished me *bon voyage* I pressed her hands to my lips. She had vanished in the crowd through the exit by the time Irmgard and Wanda emerged. 'You've missed a wonder,' I said: 'my voluntary helper.' They'd been eyeing up several, they said. Women could be so beautiful, we agreed, as with Irmgard in her FUCK THE POPE T-shirt, and Wanda in her string vest, I walked unsteadily – and uncertain of the direction – to the car park.

I drove slowly along the corniche, following their instructions.

In a side-street I drew in to the kerb. Lights, not all of them working, announced PAPILLON.

We paid our entrance-fees, walked in past two muscular, ear-ringed bouncers, and hit a wall of techno-sound. The air smelled sweetly of dope and muskily of sweat. Twenty or so couples gyrated, and others lounged against the walls or the bar. Wanda went off to get drinks. Near me, two light-brown women in army fatigues danced, pelvises thrust towards each other aggressively. Irmgard took my hands and began to twist, hips rolling easily in her loose drawstring trousers, her breasts wobbling beneath her shirt. She smiled at me from time to time but mostly her eyes scanned the bar area for Wanda.

124

The men were more concerned with their own reflections, and those on the dance floor were all shades of dark and nearly all beautiful. Freaks with dyed hair, the cross-dressers and the desiccated Afro-Caribbean Quentin Crisps, stood around the edge watching. There were a few whites, clammy-looking, *métropolitain* civil servants, I guessed, seeking the exotic. As Irmgard moved me round, I enjoyed being part of the scene. The Martinique men looked so fit, moved so beautifully – most wearing lipstick and mascara, bright shirts, a happy campiness. And then, somewhere, would come the evening's business ... I wondered where it took place – against walls, amongst the dustbins, in the public gardens, or was there too much of a risk from queer-bashers? It dawned on me as we danced that more people seemed to go into the men's toilets than came out. I'd assumed the bright-eyed flushed ones emerging had been in to take poppers to dance faster but perhaps they had just been taken.

Wanda brought us our beers, exchanged a French kiss with Irmgard, then went back to get her own drink. Irmgard and I drained our glasses in a couple of gulps, and resumed our dance. She was behind me, her hands on my waist as we danced on, sweatier and sweatier, to a sequence of old seventies disco hits. It was fun, childish fun, and I was getting less and less inhibited in my movements. A tall, burly, very black man in tight jeans and a lurex vest was chatting to Wanda; he was lighting her cigarette and laughing at something she said. At the end of the dance floor the door of the men's toilet opened again and a slim beautiful man-woman – it was almost impossible to tell – wearing tight leather trousers, a glittering tight shirt and heavy white face-powder, emerged and came up to Wanda's companion. They moved into a passionate kiss. When their mouths parted, the tall guy swung his partner around to greet Wanda.

I felt troubled ... wasn't sure ... yes, it was unmistakable, that sweet, innocent smile, the man who hated gays. Wanda was pointing, gesturing, towards us, through the swaying forest of bodies, and Juan saw me. His smile vanished. He looked as if he'd just been told he had SIDA. Wanda was leading them towards us. 'Mandy, this is Joe,' she said, and the tall black, who was clearly stoned, smiled and shook my hand; 'and this –' she stroked Juan's depilated arm – 'is Charlotte …' Staring into his powder-white face, I shook his feeble hand. Charlotte! It amused me, on top of my amusement at the situation. Drunk as I was, I sensed it was important to Juan that our acquaintance not be revealed in front of his boyfriend, so turned my attention to Joe, an ebony Kojak with nose-studs; asked him what he did; he didn't speak English and Wanda had to translate for us; he worked in a rum factory. After describing myself as a lesbian lap-dancer from Liverpool, I asked Charlotte if he'd like to dance, and drew him away.

I don't think his wide, mascara'd eyes had blinked, he was so frozen with the nightmare of this meeting. He stood almost still while I swayed in front of him. 'You could have told me you were bisexual,' I said; 'I wouldn't have minded. I'm amused by your name!' He closed his eyes and looked at the floor. 'I'm sorry,' he whispered.

'It's okay. I like diversity too. But why did you say you hated gays?'

He looked troubled. 'Why are some Jews anti-Semitic?'

Irmgard loomed up and laid a heavy hand on his shoulder, booming, with mock-anger in her voice, 'Hey, Charlotte, I want words with you! I hear you had your first pussy last night, and you never want to have another! I hear you told Joe it was like fucking a rotten mango! Now let me tell you –'

I didn't hear any more, but turned and ran, right out of the club into the sweaty night. I heard someone running after me, clomping in raised heels, and Juan-Charlotte called after me, 'Wait! Please!'

126

Reaching my car, I turned and pummelled his chest. 'You shithead! Just fuck off!' My hand shaking, I managed to unlock the car and climbed in. He kept me from shutting the door, begging me to let him explain. 'You can't drive,' he said, 'you've drunk too much. I'll get you a taxi.'

'I don't need a fucking taxi! Just shut the door and piss off, you pinko wanker!'

'Then you must let me drive you. You'll have an accident or get pulled in by the police. I've had a few drinks, but not as many as you, I would think. Please, Miranda!'

I tried to pull the door shut but he wouldn't let go. Still cursing him, I moved myself over the gear-stick to the passenger seat. He slid in, and started the car up.

I fell silent, the vibration of the car and sudden turns making me feel queasy. I think – when we had left the city far behind – I asked him why he'd fucked me, and I think he replied that I was a guest on his island, was really nice, and seemed to want it so much. That there was always the hope that it would prove enjoyable, so that he really could look for that nice, educated girl to marry, because he would like a family life and kids, but now he knew that was just a dream, and it made him feel sad. He had tears in his eyes, which he brushed away in order to see ahead; but I wasn't placated; I felt as Mont-Pelée must have done when it erupted. I couldn't bear it that I'd actually enjoyed the lovemaking with him – had wanted to repeat it. 'You used me, shitface, as an experiment,' I shouted; 'and then told your lover how fucking awful it was!'

I don't know how he would have tried to justify this, because just then I threw up all over my skirt and the floor of the Clio.

13

I CLEANED MYSELF UP with Kleenex as best I could. The vomiting fit had the effect of reducing my rage but substituting a mood of depression. Winding the window down all the way to lessen the stench, I leaned my head out and watched the darkness dream its way past me. We'd reached the bad road where the vengeful children waited, hoping that their mothers would pass. And already I could see their little eyes gleaming in the ditch. I tried to keep a grip on myself: what, after all, could they do? They were too little, too weak. I wondered if Juan could see them on his side of the road, for I was sure they were there. He was keeping his eyes intently on the winding road ahead, so probably he hadn't noticed them. I faced ahead too now, ignoring the eyes. Headlights glowed round the corner ahead; Juan strained forward, concentrating on the rain-sleeked road.

Suddenly a naked infant was up on the bonnet, staring in at me. I screamed, 'Stop!' and grabbed Juan's arm. His foot hit the brake and the car slewed, skidded, to the left before stalling. Lights reared up right in front of us and we were thrown forward against our seatbelts as a car, trying to swerve at the last moment, struck us, fortunately not head on. The other car revved up – screeched into reverse – and stopped about twenty yards down the road. One of the headlights was blanked out. We just sat, dazed. The child on the bonnet had disappeared; so had the eyes in the ditch. Only the vague shape of banana trees. The car doors ahead of us were flung open and two tall young men emerged, looked at their damaged wing, then advanced threateningly on us.

They went to the driver's side, yanked the door open and shouted Creole abuse. I got out, shaky, and stood trying not to be noticed. One of the guys, in a multicoloured T-shirt and shorts, grasped Charlotte by the shoulder and invited him to get out. He did so. Car lights and a smooth engine hum were nearing behind us, and I saw a white Citroën draw up about four car spaces behind us – what looked like an elderly white face behind the wheel. The two guys started yanking on Juan's earrings, jabbing him in the stomach, and a jeering tone entered their anger; I thought they were saying something like 'Hey, she doesn't know if she's got a cock or a cunt!' One of them grabbed him by the crotch. The jeers increased, as did the force of their jabs.

The driver of the Citroën seemed to be gesturing to me to come to him. He was white, sun-bronzed European at least – at that frightening moment I turned for succour to one of my own tribe, gratefully. I ran back to him, and he leaned out. Kindly-looking, white-haired. '*Puis-je vous aider, madame?*'

I stammered out an incoherent explanation, omitting the child, my scream, my part in the accident. '*Cette situation est très dangereuse pour vous,*' he said. '*Et pour moi aussi ce n'est pas bon. Venez!*' He leaned across to open the passenger door; assured me, as I hesitated, that he would phone the gendarmerie. I got in, sinking into soft leather, and he took off the brake, touched the accelerator and we nosed forward. The jabbing and jabbering blacks glanced indifferently at us as we drove carefully past. Juan's scared face didn't seem to be looking at anything.

Having put both cars behind us, my host lifted his car phone, and I heard him giving calm instructions as to where they would find an assault on a gay man going on. He told them to come as quickly as possible. 'My name is Bertrand,' he said to me in English after putting the phone down.

'Miranda.'

'American?'

'No, English.'

He asked where I wanted to be taken, and I told him. I sank back still further in the soft leather, feeling safe and taken care of. His gentle voice and manner reminded me of my father.

His family, he said, had lived on the island for over two hundred years. He was in the banana business. I told him I was a lecturer living in London, and we talked about that city, which he had visited a couple of times and enjoyed.

The man guarding the barrier at the hotel sprang up and to salute with more deference than usual. Outside the reception, Bertrand shook my hand, told me to get a good night's sleep, and wished me good luck. I thanked him profusely.

The male receptionist looked with curiosity at my stained skirt. He handed me a message along with my key. It was from Yvette, telling me that Jean-Pierre had died, and thanking me for my kind support and help. She would call me again when I was home.

In my room, I stripped and was asleep within minutes.

I awoke the next morning quite late, with a throbbing head. I took a couple of Resolves, consumed a litre of mineral water, showered, and sank back on the bed with a cigarette. Only now did I allow myself to remember Juan and the accident. I felt guilt at leaving him to his fate; though not too much. I recalled 'like fucking a rotten mango' ... I went to the restaurant for coffee and a croissant, and afterwards called the breakdown emergency number on my car hire agreement. Reported an accident about five miles from Trois Ilets, and said the car was still there. A polite woman said they'd been informed by the gendarmes, and it had already been driven to Jumbocar, near my hotel. I should go there.

The damage was minor. I shouldn't have let anyone else drive it, but she understood I'd had little choice. She couldn't say if I'd have to pay for the damages. Probably not.

What had happened to the driver? I asked. She didn't know. I thanked her, and rang off. I lay back down, and fell into a deep sadness. I cried. Not for Juan, nor Yvette, nor even myself – but for that pale, gaunt cow I had glimpsed several times in a ditch by a road. I felt its loneliness, its bewilderment.

I roused myself to go for a coffee and a swim. After the swim, back in my room, I felt in a dreamy state, and spent a long time painting my nails. I had finished one hand when the phone rang. I heard a Creole babble, gathered it was Joe, Juan's boyfriend, and asked him to slow down and speak clearly. Juan had asked him to call me, he said, to make sure I'd got back safely.

'Yes, I'm fine; how is he?'

'They roughed him up a bit, but no broken bones.'

'I was scared they'd rape him.'

'They probably would have, if their car hadn't been damaged. They wanted to make sure he'd have to pay for it, so they called the police on a mobile.'

I said the old guy who'd given me a lift had called them too. 'That's why I went with him, Joe – to make sure the police were called.' Joe said I'd done the right thing, and Juan thought so too. He was having a sleep now, after a night in the cells.

'In the cells? Why?'

'He was over the limit.'

'Oh, fuck … What's likely to happen to him?'

A fine and a driving ban. But the worst was, he'd lose his job. His homosexuality would be revealed in court; he'd be asked to resign.

'He must hate me. He wanted to put me in a cab, but I wouldn't let him.'

131

'He shouldn't have screwed you, sweetheart, he knows that.'
Nor talked to him about it, I said; but I was very sorry, and to tell
him that. I asked if Juan had always called himself Charlotte.

'No, he's always been Juanita. He was so proud of the book you
gave him, by this Charlotte woman.' His voice became a degree
more unfriendly. 'Why do you think he made his face up to be
white? He wanted to be you, he admired you. Anyway, I've got to
get to work. Safe flight.'

I finished my nails. I would email Juan from home. Yvette, I
thought, might know someone who could get him a teaching post
in France – mainland France. Surely, as a gay, he'd be happier
there. I'd talk to her about it, once she'd recovered a little.

I put on a dress over my bikini, and wandered down to Jumbocar, taking my tape recorder with me. The big-breasted, cheerful
woman who had served me before was sympathetic. I'd have to
leave my deposit with them, but she'd try her best to get it
refunded. And, yes, they had a car I could take for today. I got into
another, older Clio, and drove towards Les Anses.

The beach was deserted except for Jerry. He seemed very
pleased I was alone this time. No one else was around; soon he'd
be out of work. We took a swim together, then went to his hut.
He was now quite willing – eager indeed – to bite me all over, but
I stopped him. Fresh bite-marks would take some explaining …
'The mosquitos are enormous …' I wouldn't get away with it. Jerry
certainly had no qualms about not using a condom. I knew it was
dangerous, but what the fuck; we all had to die of something.

We had a beer, I went for another swim, and – when he was
busy serving a French family that had turned up – slipped away.
Under a pile of franc coins I left a note saying, 'I'm flying home
tonight. I think I love you, Jerry – it's been great.' Of course it
wasn't true, but I thought it might boost his morale.

Glancing at my watch, I have a sudden impulse to drive north, up into the hills where I saw the butterflies. I can do it in under an hour.

I drive fast. The pale, skeletal cow passes in a flash. *Vitesse tue* … For once the *autoroute* near the airport isn't clogged with traffic. Finally I am out into the quieter, forested, mountainous landscape of the north.

I'm driving higher and higher, and there's the sign to the Gauguin house, which I never found, and don't particularly wish to; and here's the quiet narrow road where I picked up the cane-worker, and I glance at my watch and I'm in good time. I pull in near the lonely bus-stop, switch off the engine, and wait.

In my rear mirror I see him coming: heavy, sweaty, dragging his machete. As he comes close, looking uncertain – the car's different – I lean out and say to him with a smile, *'Bonsoir, Luc!'* He beams at me: *'Ah, bonsoir, Madame Charlotte!'* As he moves around the back of the car to get in, I reach behind me to press the record button. He opens the door and heaves his bulk in.

'So damn hot, Charlotte' – grabbing tissues to wipe his face.

'Yes.'

We drove to the same spot where one could pull off the road into a small clearing.

As he fucked me, grunting, his heavy sweaty belly pressing against me, I recited to him, in my father's fruity Home Counties burr, *Drake's Drum*. Understanding scarcely a word, Luc loved it, or loved my voice. Afterwards I drove him to his little shack. I could see two small black faces pressed to the window. 'Are they your kids?'

'No, my girl's. I have a lovely boy on St Lucia.'

'What did your girl say about me?'

'She feel proud of me. Her man could get a lovely white woman.'

'Take care.'

133

I drove lazily south again. I could feel the spunk of the two islanders mixed up together in my cunt, and it was good. I bought gifts in Trois Ilets – a bright dress for Alison, shirts for David and Jeremy. Back in the cool of my room, I called home. David, who answered, sounded harassed and tetchy. 'The loo in the main bathroom's blocked.'

'Oh, shit!'

'Literally.'

'That's Jeremy, I bet. He always has problems with his bowels when exams are coming up. Have you rung a plumber?'

We discussed plumbers, their non-availability, for a while, then he asked me how things had gone. I told him okay, only it was too damn hot; today I'd had to drive up into the hills, to get a little cooler; I'd seen a house Gauguin once lived in, not very interesting.

'What time do you arrive at Heathrow?'

'Nine-thirty, if it's on time. Could you order a minicab to meet me?'

'Will do.'

I gave him the flight number from Paris. He softened his voice: 'I've missed you, Andy ...' It's been his pet name for me ever since we coined it at college as a way of misleading his wife. 'It'll be good to –'

'Yes it will! Can't wait ... I had a message from Yvette; Jean-Pierre died.'

'I'm sorry.' And he's such a nice guy, he sounded as if he meant it. I asked him if there were any messages. 'Lyn rang just now,' he said, 'she thought you'd be back today. One of your students o.d.'d. Samantha Smith?'

'Christ.'

'I think she's going to be okay. Your shrink faxed to say he won't be able to see you next week; he has a conference in Stockholm.'

134

'Bastard.'

'Marcus and Helen want us to play tennis on Sunday afternoon; I said okay.'

'Fine.'

When we'd rung off I sat for a while, feeling empty and depressed. I didn't believe Theo had a conference to go to all of a sudden; he was punishing me for taking this week off. It was so petty, so immature of him. Or maybe he'd got my card saying I was flirting with two men, and was angry; though it was unlikely he'd got it so soon. I took the box of cigars I'd bought for him out of my overnight case, opened it, broke the cigars in half, and dumped box and cigar pieces into the waste bin.

I wondered how crowded the road to the airport would be, and how easy it would be to find the Jumbocar office in the dark. I was cutting it fine, but couldn't get myself going.

Suddenly – as clearly as Jane heard a voice call, 'Jane! Jane! Jane!' – I heard my mother call, 'Mandy – time to get going, you'll be late!' The tone she used when I dawdled in my bedroom before school – not wanting, Theo says, to leave my parents there in case they rowed violently. Now I felt she was just outside the door. It happens maybe once a year, still. It always upsets me, the clarity of that voice after so many years, and I reached for the tissues.

I had an impulse to call my father. It would be almost eleven, there in Cornwall, but he stayed up late. Probably with the dictaphone, recording the day's non-events for his journal. Alice had said he had a very bad cold; I wanted to hear his voice. I lifted the phone, but got a disengaged tone. I realised it was past my late-checkout time. I'd call him from home tomorrow, and arrange a visit in two or three weeks. He would like that. He was lonely.

Stuffing my toilet and make-up bags into my case, I zipped it up. A tap at the door. I went to open it, thinking it was a maid wanting to clean up. But it was a male form that loomed above me in the gathering murk: Jerry, his wide mouth grinning. I backed away in surprise, and he came in. Laying his brawny hands on my shoulders, he said: 'I loved your note. There's no need to cry any more, I'm here. What does age matter? Dry your eyes, *doudou*. We'll get married, okay? My big *lapin* is yours forever.'

Reader, I told him to piss off.

14

Friday June 25th

Miranda arrives by taxi from Penzance. I know I must savour every precious moment of this weekend, because it will be the last time I see her. She flings herself into my arms as she did when a schoolgirl. I draw away to look at her closely, and she is so achingly like Emma; every passing year draws her closer to Emma. And her hair, long, straight, jet black – as I draw my hand down over it to her shoulder I can believe it is her mother's.

The taxi-driver – I've known him for years – clambers out. 'Evenin', Mr Stevenson!'

'Evening, Gary!'

He carries her case inside, evidently thinking me too frail. My daughter pays him and he drives away back over the Penwith moor. She takes my arm, and draws me to the top of Eagle's Nest. It's a day of blustery wind – when is it not? – but the scudding clouds are high. She's taking deep breaths, gazing out at what is a greyish blur to me; but I know she is looking at all the tiny grey-green Celtic fields, the shimmering aquamarine sea, the beloved hamlet with its church tower.

'It's good to breathe real air again, Daddy!'

'Some diffr'n from Lunnon, you, in 'a?' I say in my mock Cornish voice.

''Es, some diffr'n, you!' We laugh, and the years since she lived here fall away.

We turn back, arm in arm, towards the house. I can hear Mrs Tregonning's voice greeting her with, 'Mandy! My lover, how 'ee doin'?' And Miranda lets go my arm to greet her at the kitchen door. 'I'm fine, Alice! How are you?'

'Oh, I can't complain. I've got my nephew Colin and his family comin' down to stay next month; that'll be nice.'

'It will be. Lovely to see you again! I hope my Dad's not been treating you too badly!' She draws me to her again, and I can see her bewitching, laughing face.

'Oh, he've been a proper tyrant!' She cackles. 'I'm glad his bronchitis have cleared up, though; I was a bit worried. He's some pleased to see you. I expected you to be burnt black, my sweetheart.'

'A tan doesn't last long in London, Alice.'

'You're lookin' well though. I've got pasties in the oven – do 'ee think you can tackle one, later?'

'Ooh, that's a real luxury!'

'She doesn't get gourmet food like your pasties in London, Alice,' I flatter and flutter her.

Miranda excuses herself to go and freshen up. I know she will be taking her time, familiarising herself afresh with everything that has not changed for thirty years. The rows and rows of unread Victorian minor poets, on the landing bookshelves, the pictures from the Newlyn School of long-aproned women helping with the nets, of schoolmistresses in dingy schoolrooms, of sorrowful maidens holding distressing letters. The old wedding photos, and the later photos of the three of us.

She joins me in the dining room, just as Mrs Tregonning puts the pasties on the table, along with a big pot of tea, and (with a wink at my daughter) the sugar bowl. 'I do remember you like sugary tea with your pasty! Still a proper Cornish girl!'

'Yes, Alice!'

The Cornish mostly gave up sugar to support the abolition movement; but kept it for their precious pasties. It was something I learned from Emma when I married her.

Alice bade us goodnight. I can see the glow of a candle and not much else; but I hear my daughter's voice, and that is enough. She talks to me about the children. She knows I feel hurt that I've seen nothing of them for four years. She puts into my hands a leather-bound book, the first French translation of *Vanity Fair*, which she says she was surprised to find in Martinique. I lean across to kiss her cheek, saying I will look at it carefully in the morning light.

There is also a bottle of white rum. She has brought herbs, she says, with which to make a drink she thinks I will enjoy. But perhaps not after pasty!

We sit in the bay window. She can see all the way down to Pendeen; the June light is still good enough, at nine, for the Pendeen Light not to shine out.

'Will you play for me?' she asks; and I say, 'If you will sing.' I sit at the piano – apologising because it could do with tuning – and move into the old ballads. 'Macoushla ...' 'Only a Rose ...' 'Pale hands I loved, beside the Shalimar ...' Her voice is not so pure and sweet as her mother's, I tell her, because she does not use it, but with the same timbre. Now and again I add my gravelly old voice to hers. It is a magical hour.

While she is upstairs having a pee, the phone rings. It's her wanker of a husband, bringing the evening's first jarring note. 'Hello, Ben: is Andy there?' he says; and I reply curtly, 'Miranda's here, yes.' I can just about tolerate Mandy, but I can't find any hope of salvation in a man who distorts her name so atrociously.

'David,' I say, holding the phone for her as she comes downstairs. I sit back in the bay window, her voice almost out of earshot; but I hear enough to know they are having a disagreement. When she comes off the phone, and sits by me, I observe, 'You are not getting on very well.'

'No.' She relights my cigar and has a cigarette herself. 'I don't know what's going to happen. We may split up, I don't know.'

'There's always room for you here, you know; and for the children.'

'I know that, Daddy, and it's very kind of you; but I have my job, and they have their schools.'

'Ah, yes – *schools*!' She knows what I think of that. They drain all the life, all the originality, out of you; I thank God I avoided them, and taught myself, surrounded by Dickens, Thackeray, Trollope, and so on, in my uncle's library.

'Let's not quarrel,' she says, and moves from her armchair to sit on my lap. The cool silk feel of her white dress; the perfume that I recognise with joy as *Fleurs de Rocailles*. I ask her, won't she read to me from her Martinique journal, which she's mentioned over the phone. Tomorrow perhaps, she says; she's too tired now. Only it's no longer a journal, more of a story.

'Marvellous.'

'Only I haven't changed the names yet. I can't decide what to call myself.'

Night falls; she can see the Pendeen Light, she says, happily. How many nights, in the past, when she could hear the foghorn boom too. And so to bed – kissing outside her bedroom door, as we used to do. As she shuts her door, I remember how often the poor girl had to push her chest of drawers against it, when her mother was in one of her angry, violent moods.

After I've cooked us bacon and eggs – fresh, free-range eggs, not the rubbish she's used to – we set out for our usual walk on the moors. It's chilly, with occasional drenching showers; huge sackfuls of dark clouds are being driven from the Atlantic, but there are moments of warm sunshine too. On this toe of England, both coasts only a few miles apart, the weather is always active, energetic, surprising, improvisational, at one with the stony cairns and the sea. Up here my lack of vision doesn't matter so much; I've drawn the whole bleak landscape into me, the rain, the rocks, the isolated old engine-houses of the mines, the Bronze Age tombs: it's all here, within me.

And I can still see the healthy glow in her cheeks, when we return from our walk. Alice is here, tidying up; she only comes for two hours of a Saturday. She makes us a pot of coffee, and shows Miranda what's in the fridge. Steaks for tonight.

Miranda changes out of her shorts and walking-boots. Her dress is too short, I tell her – almost up to her arse. She says I always told her that and I say, Yes, and you never took any notice! – and then took your revenge on me by wearing jeans and overalls!

We take the track down through the bracken into Zennor. There are, as yet, not too many cars parked around the church and the pub. In a few weeks, you won't be able to get near it, with the eclipse adding to the normal high season overcrowding. We climb the steps into the little graveyard, and to Emma's grave. Miranda removes the faded flowers and carefully arranges the fresh hydrangeas; then we stand together for a few moments, looking at the stone. The letters are beginning to fade. She says I should get Jack Penhallow to refresh the lettering; she will pay for it. I say: Why waste money? Wait till I'm put here too.

'Well, Daddy,' she says, after another reflective silence, 'she did literally dance on her grave.'

'She certainly did.' My voice almost breaks. How is it I feel such sorrow after twenty-five years? Yes, she danced on her own grave, my God she did! How many times, that phone call from the pub: four, five? – the embarrassed voice saying, 'Ben, it's Ted ... we've got Emma here; Elsie is looking after her ...' 'Okay, I'll be right down.' And there would be Emma, when I went in the back way, sitting with a blanket round her, smiling innocently-cunningly at me, asking what all the fuss was about – she was only dancing in the nude, in the dark, on her own, not troubling anyone, everyone had filthy minds.

And a couple of times, she went in the 'Tinners' Arms' herself, silencing the hymn-singing and talk and laughter, going around and sitting on men's laps, asking them if they wanted to fuck, and referring to when they'd done it before; and no doubt some of them had. But it was her illness; manic depression does that.

And Miranda, in her bedroom, hearing me bring her home, and often Emma struggling and not wanting to be brought in, calling me a cunt and a prick for keeping her chained up. Then having to deal with the sniggers at school. Not easy for her.

We enter the small, dim, beautiful old church. She wants to light a candle. Then we go to the mermaid's pew. I can no longer see the carving in the dim light – indeed, in here it's as if I'm totally blind; but I trace it with my fingers. The mermaid combing her long hair, looking at herself in the mirror. Planning to sing to Matthew Trewella, tenor, so sweetly and seductively that he would follow her down to the sea, and be lost with her, in her.

In the pub she greets the up-country landlord, Charles, and orders our sandwiches. We take our drinks into a corner. She's brought with her the paper she presented in Martinique, and she reads it to me. I like it, I tell her. She's a bright girl. She ought to be at an Oxbridge college, teaching literature; this Women's Studies stuff she's in is all nonsense; and really she knows it.

She knows the Victorians so well. I saw to that. She was lucky, as she says – she had the Bodleian all around her, books crammed everywhere, even piled up in the bathroom! I must have given her *Jane Eyre* to read when she was eight or nine. I told her they had a Cornish mother, the Brontë sisters.

As if reading my mind, she says, smiling, 'Do you remember when we were in Lloyds Bank, Penzance, and we heard a little old lady at one of the tills say, "My name is Branwell!" – and you whispered to me, "She must be a descendant of the Brontës!" '

I nod. 'You were in your Grammar School uniform. You had pigtails, I recall.'

Our plates are removed; her eyes are sparkling like the cider. She asks me to remind her how that poem goes, the John Heath-Stubbs, about Zennor. I frown, concentrate; my memory isn't what it was; I can only find, in the crammed, musty, uncatalogued library of my weakening mind, the second verse ...

> *This is a hideous and a wicked country,*
> *Sloping to hateful sunsets and the end of time,*
> *Hollow with mine-shafts, naked with granite, fanatic*
> *With sorrow. Abortions of the past*
> *Hop through these bogs; black-faced, the villagers*
> *Remember burnings by the hewn stones ...*

Her eyes are closed; she's in a trance. A happy one, I think; or at least with a mixture of sorrow and happiness, which is the best we can look for in life. 'It's so true,' she murmurs.

'Written by a blind man.'

'Yes. Is he still alive?'

'I've no idea.'

143

The sun is out, when we emerge. By instinct and long custom, we turn left into the lanes that lead to Zennor Head. We leave people behind, and cars; the silence grows deeper and deeper as we follow the line of the cliff. Wildflowers, bracken, sea, sky: nothing else. We find a flattish rock to sit on.

And this spot, almost exactly, was where ...

I've been building up to this moment. I say to her I don't want her to be too upset, but this is probably going to be the last time we see each other. I don't want to become a burden on anyone. I intend coming here on August 11th, the day of the total eclipse; and at the moment when the moon completely blocks out the sun, I shall follow her mother.

She becomes panic-stricken, as I anticipated; she cries hysterically; she can't take *another* suicide. But I say it's more like euthanasia; I've had my day, I'm almost blind, I've lost my libido; women, as in the pub, look at me as an object of pity. And she says I've *not* lost my libido, or my attractiveness, I will never lose that, because of the power of my mind – 'You're Picasso!' she says. 'And you're *not* going to do this to me! I think you're making a black joke to upset me; don't fuck with me, Daddy!'

'I'm not fucking with you; what is there left for me?'

'*Me!*'

'You! I hardly ever see you. You're away all of August; where is it this year? A villa in Tuscany?'

She nods, wiping her eyes; mumbles about its depending on her and David, what's going to happen between them.

'Of course, I could come with you,' I say, rather spitefully, knowing it is out of the question. She buries her head in her hands. 'I wish you could, but –'

'– David won't allow it! He thinks I'm going to molest his precious little Ali! God, when I think of that!'

'It's different generations, Daddy. For you it was just tickling

144

your little granddaughter at bath-time; but these days, it's different. *I* know there was nothing sexual in it, but –'

I shout, 'Of *course* it was sexual! Everything in the world is sexual! Of *course* tickling her little pussy was sexual! But it wasn't harmful! I used to tickle your little puss at bath-time, and so did your Mum: did it do you any harm?'

'No. No.'

'Christ! My uncle's nanny used to suck his little widdler to put him to sleep! Back in the Victorian Age! He told me so. All the nannies did ... David's an idiot, a sour little puritan. But you backed him up, and stopped me seeing my grandchildren. If you loved me you'd never have allowed it.'

She turns to me and hammers her fists against my chest. 'You bastard! You know I love you!'

'All right, all right, calm down!' I take her arms and lower them, and put my arms around her. She is sobbing, whispering, she can't bear the thought of my dying, I must promise ... So I promise. I kiss away the salt tears on her cheeks as I have done so many times.

We walk home, quietly, up the slope.

Feeling exhausted, she goes to have a lie-down. I sit in the armchair listening to my favourite Kathleen Ferrier LPs, the Alto Rhapsody and English folk songs. Nothing evokes Emma's singing voice so strongly, not even Miranda's; though of course Ferrier's is incomparably finer. But the rich tone, the soulfulness ...

I drowse in the armchair; I don't hear her approach. She puts her arms around me and kisses my forehead. She looks brighter, fresher, happier; she's in her bathrobe. 'I'm going to take a bath now,' she says, 'and then dress for dinner. I'm not sure what to wear this evening. Would you like to come up in twenty minutes or so to tell me what you think?'

'Yes, gladly.' I kiss her hand.

I hear the rumble of the bath-water running. After a few minutes I climb the stairs and go into my bedroom. I sit in the cane chair before the dressing-table, still with Emma's perfumes and other items on it. I wait. The weather has darkened again, and drizzle brushes the small-paned window. I switch on the lamp. She will need light to dress by.

She enters, smiles at me. 'That was lovely!' Goes to the wardrobe, the womanly side. 'Now what do you think?' she asks.

'Oh, the black; you look good in it.'

'Black always looks nice, doesn't it?'

She takes out the black dress on its hanger, hooks it onto the wardrobe door. She pulls open a drawer of the chest of drawers and ruffles through underwear, choosing. Lays the chosen garments on top. Now she slips out of her bathrobe, unselfconsciously, saying, 'I'm glad we're eating in tonight, the weather's turned foul,' and I say, 'Yes, it's nasty.' She snakes around her the black suspender belt – it must be older than Miranda, but still good; she strains to fasten it, whereas it used to be a bit loose on her; she has put on some weight around the middle. The bra fits, as always. She steps into and pulls up the panties. She takes the dress off the hanger and steps into it. Stands close with her back to me. 'Would you zip me up?' I stand to do so, making sure to fasten the little hook-and-eye at the top.

She goes to the drawer again. She takes out two packets of stockings. The stockings were bought for her only a year or so ago. Emma's, alas, all became laddered. 'Seamed or unseamed?'

'The seamed, I think, Emma, don't you?' Genuine, vintage, ordered from a special shop in Romford.

'They're more stylish.'

She opens the packet and draws out the fine fully-fashioned black nylons. 'Light me a cigarette, will you, Ben? They're in my robe pocket.'

I take out her Silk Cut and light her one. She takes it between her fine, slim fingers, draws in deeply then places it on an ash-tray on the dressing-table. Sitting on the double bed, she draws the gossamer over her hand and carefully starts to roll the stocking up her leg; rucking back her dress, draws down the suspenders and fastens them, giving the straps a last tightening pull. After another puff of her cigarette, she starts on the other stocking.

The pattering rain, and wind rattling the window; the subdued light; the cigarette like a wandering star; the womanly scent: sad-sweet memories of Eros. Or not memories quite; neither memory nor present reality; a blend of both ... 'You have beautiful legs, Emma; does Peter compliment you on them?'

Immediately she recognises which of the 'Emma' variations I've chosen, and moves subtly – it only needs to be subtle – into her mother's soft Cornish tones, murmuring, 'He d'say my thighs are very soft; do 'ee think they are?'

'Beautifully soft.'

'He d'like to kiss them – just here – while he runs his hand down under my stockin'.'

Rising, cigarette in hand, she approaches the bed, turning her back to me. 'Are my seams straight?' I have to get to my knees, like a supplicant, to see; though mostly I check by touch, the seams, the tension of the back suspenders. 'Yes, they're fine.'

She goes to the wardrobe again, and finds the black high heels. 'How do I look, Daddy?'

'Wonderful, Miranda ... Now I'm going to make myself look decent.'

She sits at the dressing-table, searching through make-up.

After bathing, I put on a clean white shirt and my twenty-year-old suit. I hear Dusty Springfield singing downstairs; a clatter of dishes in the kitchen.

When I come downstairs, there's a delicious smell; she tells me how smart I look – brushing some minute dust particle off my lapel. I can open the wine, she tells me. But first she offers me a rum cocktail and we clink glasses.

The table is resplendently laid. A red table cloth. Tall green candles burn, and there's a scent of incense.

It's a simple meal, the kind I like. Smoked salmon, steak, a cheeseboard. Dusty has been replaced by Elgar's Serenade for Strings, ultimate English nostalgia and yearnful sadness. But we are not sad this evening; we sparkle, tell jokes; she entertains me with Martinique lesbians and other absurdities. Emma, shadowily looking down at us – the portrait by Lamorna Birch – wouldn't disapprove. In her good times, which were many, how she could sparkle!

What was her most poignant memory of Martinique? I ask her. A cow, she replies unexpectedly; a gaunt cow lying day after day in a roadside ditch.

The phone's ringing breaks in on us. 'It's probably David,' she says; 'leave it – unless you're expecting a call from someone?'

'No. You're the only one who ever calls me these days. So why the quarrel with David; what's it about?'

The ringing stops.

'I went a bit wild on Martinique.'

'Splendid! You slept with someone?'

'I slept with four men, actually.'

I let out a chortle of delight. 'My God, Miranda! That's incredible! You're living at last!'

'Or not slept with, but screwed. I had to tell David, because I'm pregnant.'

I choke on my wine. She continues, 'It could be one of two men: a mute young beach waiter, tall, good-looking and thick, or an even thicker middle-aged cane-worker I gave a lift to. The other

148

two used condoms; one of them turned out to be a raving queer; it's an amusing story.'

I become agitated at the thought that, with the others, she had not made them wear condoms; these West Indian islands are rife with AIDS. She assures me they were clean; she could tell. Her assurance fails to assure me; but what can one do?

'Were they black?' I ask her.

'As the ace of spades.'

I can't help laughing – warmed by the food, the rum, the wine, and above all, David's come-uppance. 'I'm sorry, darling, I know it's no laughing matter. So what are you going to do?'

'David wants me to have an abortion, but I won't.'

'Good for you! He was a right bastard, making you have one before. He was never any good for you. You should have left him years ago, but you'd never listen to me.'

'I only told him about the cane-worker. I felt *one* was quite enough for him to deal with. This guy had his machete with him in the car; David wanted me to say he'd threatened me, I'd felt terrified, so it was rape. I wouldn't say it. I said I'd wanted it as much as him. Of course David was crying.'

'Of course.'

'I told him I wasn't going to contribute to the stereotype of blacks being rapists, by lying.'

'Good for you!'

'He kept trying to find some excuse for me. That being in an exotic place made it more understandable – but I said it *wasn't* exotic, it was just France – the EU ... Daddy, I want this baby, I really do! I want it!'

'Then, let's drink a toast!' I grab the bottle and move round the table to refill her glass. Her eyes are wide-open, shining. 'I really do want it!'

'Then bloody have it! Live! Do it your own way! Like I said, you can always come here.'

'Thank you. I have to work out what's best. I offered to take a sabbatical and go off to Africa or somewhere for six months; then come back with a baby we could say we're adopting. An orphan. Because otherwise it *will* be difficult for the kids to accept.'

'That's true.'

'I don't want to humiliate them – or him. Everybody knows he's had a vasectomy, so, even if it weren't black or brown ...' She spread her arms. David, she continues, left home for a couple of days, but then thought about giving up the house and the kids, and being in the position he was with his other son, whom he never sees these days. So he came back and is sleeping in the spare room while they decide what to do.

'Well!' I say, with something of a chortle. 'Who'd have believed it! ... I want to know all about these ... encounters.'

'In detail,' she says with a smile. She knows me well.

'Everything.'

So she tells me. And I have that feeling, a strange mixture of intense jealousy and intense excitement, I had when Emma would goad me and rouse me with some man or other. But alive ... certainly alive. And Miranda knows it. 'You're a wicked old man,' she says; 'you're Picasso!'

Then it's brandy and coffee, a cigar and a cigarette. She says how good it feels to be here; how free she feels. Perhaps she *will* come here. She's had enough of academia; she'd like to write fiction. She has an idea for creating alternative endings to nineteenth-century novels – to bring out some of the repressed issues. She thinks *Jane Eyre*, *Pride & Prejudice*, and perhaps *Mill on the Floss*. My mind springs to the most precious manuscript in my collection, one that she was responsible for getting for me;

150

and of course I know it must be in her mind too – probably even inspired her idea.

She says it will help her make a start, because she won't have to invent an entirely new plot. I encourage her in her ambitions. She's bloody bright, I tell her, and I'm proud of her. Her mother would be proud of her too. She says, she's going to need my help, so I'd better not fucking die!

Leaning forward, her arms on the table, serious, she says: 'I have a moral problem about the *Jane Eyre*; I need your advice. I'd like to start out from Charlotte's own alternative ending. If it *is* hers.'

'It is; and you must. No question.'

(God, how like her mother she is, in her calm times, serious, intelligent, lighting a cigarette, the candle flame dancing in her hair!)

'Yes, but there's the promise to Nicholls' great-niece.'

The cigarette held close to her lush lips – just as in that snap I took, one of the first I took of her, 1954, my first holiday in Cornwall ... and saw that enchanting young woman serving in the ice cream parlour by St Ives harbour ...

'She must be long dead, darling. She wanted the money to help her move into a private nursing home, right? She can't be still alive.'

Nodding, breathing smoke out: 'But that leaves the problem, if I declare Charlotte's part-authorship, everyone's going to think me dotty, and the vultures will come after the manuscript. But if I don't declare it, it's a kind of theft.'

'An innocent theft. And you'll change some of it?'

'Of course; I want to take up where she left off; but also, naturally, make some changes in what she wrote ... Yes, that's what I'll do. Thank you.' She smiles roguishly. 'I'm going to take her to Martinique!'

'Hah! Jean would have loved that!'

151

'Did you fuck her, Daddy?'

'You'll have to wait for my journals. Edit them when I'm gone.'

'Okay.'

I play the piano again, and she sings. 'The Floral Dance ...' 'Bess, you is my woman now ...' (Not inappropriate, as we laughingly agree!) She washes up, while I go on tinkling away. The phone rings. I pick it up. That poncy voice, strained-sounding, asking for 'Andy'.

'Miranda's not here,' I say; 'she's dining with an old friend in St Ives, Sebastian Jarvis; I think she'll be back very late.' He knows who Jarvis is, a mediocre but rather sexy artist. Miranda used to tease him about Jarvis. Fuck him! Does he think I'm going to screw his precious girl? What is this fucking puritan, politically correct modern world, where it's fine to fuck a dozen men up the bum in a bath-house but you can't make your own granddaughter giggle with a tickle of her little *patate*? (A Creole term, rather nice, which Miranda shares with me.)

It's time for bed. I tell her it's been the best evening I've had for years. 'Let me give you something,' she says, and goes to pick up her briefcase and flick it open. She takes from it a couple of ring binders and brings them to me, a sudden shy look on her face. 'Actually I've just about finished the *Jane Eyre*,' she says. 'It's the exam period, so I've had some time. Would you read it when I'm gone, Daddy?'

'With great pleasure!' I open the first of them. I see she has thoughtfully used a large-sized font. I pick up my magnifying glass. 'Ah, so you're Jennifer Trefusis, are you! Tired of your old Dad's name?'

(She has always remained Miranda Stevenson, sensibly shuddering at the thought of being Mrs Miranda Foulkes.)

I sense that she blushes. She just thinks she should distinguish the creative writer from the academic; and Trefusis, Emma's maiden name, has a good ring to it. Yes, I agree, it's a beautiful name, though I harbour the suspicion that this is a slightly distancing gesture. Well, it's understandable.

We climb the stairs; separate briefly, then she comes and carries out the ritual of undressing and putting the clothes neatly away. Those that don't need washing. Mrs Tregonning – Miranda thinks it quaint I still often call Alice that, when years ago we were *intime* – will give the nylons a hand-wash. A last cigarette, a last short variation from my memory's audio-library. Slips into her robe. Then gives me a hug and a kiss before she leaves.

We have never crossed the forbidden frontier.

I am shaken out of a deep sleep; Miranda, her eyes glaring inches from mine, is gripping and shaking me and shouting, 'You ask me to edit your fucking journals! You expect me to go through all that horror! You're a fucking rapist, a mind-rapist!' And much more of the same, mad, unreal: how I'd drowned her, as I drowned her mother; how she existed underwater, like a submarine; how all those years alone with me made it impossible for her to find a different life. 'This will be *our* child, you know that, don't you!' From her robe pocket she takes scissors, Emma's, and holds them to my throat like a dagger. Her robe is unfastened, her naked breasts hovering before me: but I can see only her wild, violent eyes and the scissors, listen to her vomit of abuse. Before I can escape from the shock she is sitting back, smiling affectionately; kisses me on the brow murmuring, 'Sleep well, Daddy!' Flits from the room. I am deeply, deeply shaken – excited too, in a weird way – yet fall back asleep.

Sunday June 27th

To church. Miranda in the pale pink suit, so stylish, with white court shoes and Aristoc fleshtone with the cuban heels. So proud to sit with her. But the Anglican service is all fucked-up, the poetry gone. Then to the pub for lunch. Sad to be walking back, knowing she must go soon. No mention of the night. A dream, then. With Emma, dream and reality often became confused.

Changed into her travelling gear (which always means scruffy, these days), she brings her case down. Hands me a tiny gift-wrapped package. 'This might give you some entertainment when I'm gone.'

'You're too good to me.' I put it down on the hall-table so I can embrace her. We hear the sound of the taxi coming up the lane. I ask her if she has a good book for the journey, and she says she wants to write a long letter. She won't tell me to whom; she is a curious mixture of the frank and the secretive.

It's Gary again in the cab; he leaps out. 'It's been a great weekend,' she says as he stows her case in the boot. 'I'll see you very soon. I may not go to Tuscany; or I might join them halfway through. In any case, I'll be here with you when the sun mates with the moon.'

'Goodbye, darling.'

I am left to this vast, crumbling house, these fucking books. There is all this blather she gives me about sheltered housing – company – whether in Cornwall or Blackheath. But what would I do with all these books, these paintings?

I have her manuscript to read. But first I take from the safe the slightly-yellowed Charlotte Brontë original, and read it. It invariably moves me. At first, that New York woman I was so struck on – her name has gone for the moment – thought it was my daughter's doing, because she was clearly jealous: as if a girl just out of pigtails and 'A' levels and gym slips could have created twelve elegant pages in Brontë's hand! The silly woman even accused her of trying to stir up trouble between us – on the grounds that the 'alternative' last chapter hinted the Rochester-Jane marriage might not turn out well! But then that graphologist, comparing it with my – undoubtedly authentic – C.B. letter to Thackeray, said it was one and the same handwriting, no question. And the ink, and the paper ...

Not that *I* needed the word of technical 'experts'. Now, reading it for about the hundredth time, I am more certain than ever. I think after a couple of years at Bletchley Park, twelve successful years working in the Bodleian, and forty in the antiquarian book trade, I can spot a fraud!

After locking it away again, I sit in the bay window and start out on my daughter's writings. I soon see she has done a good job expanding on Brontë's own second thoughts (or were they her first thoughts? ...) Of course it's now evidently *pastiche* Brontë, not the absolute crystal-clear authenticity of the original; but still ...

I sit for hours. Dusk is falling when I put the ring binder aside to go and open a tin of soup. She should be home by now; I ring their number, but get David's pompous answerphone message ('Neither David nor Miranda Foulkes is available to speak to you at the moment, but ...'). I ask her to call me when she gets in. After wolfing the soup I return to the bay window.

It's midnight, I'm nodding off, when the phone rings. She sounds tired, poor dear. The journey back was okay, she says – only, almost as long as it took to get to Martinique. She's sorry she hasn't rung before, but she and David have been discussing matters. 'We're splitting up, Daddy. He doesn't want to move out, because of the kids, and he could never afford anywhere in Blackheath or Greenwich. Prices are shooting up on account of the Dome. So I've said he can have the big room on the third floor – which we were thinking of letting – turned into a bedsit.'

'I think it's the right decision.'

'He's in his study howling. The kids say he's been crying and acting very strangely all weekend. I think he's having a breakdown.' Of course it's also to do with his work, she adds; he can think of nothing to put in the Faith Zone.

'My dear, anyone as unfailingly rational and PC as David is bound to have a breakdown sometime; because life isn't like that. Life's more like your mother.'

'Mad!'

'Well, yes. And surprising and beautiful.'

'You don't think I'm being cruel, do you – confining him to one upstairs room?'

'Not at all. Find him a Grace Poole.'

I hear a splurge of laughter; then – 'Oh, Dad, that's awful!'

'Sorry. No, seriously, it's kind of you.'

'I hope so. He says he can't stand the thought of being completely alone again, after so many years. It reminded me of something Juan said about Martinique: that it wouldn't be able to cope with independence now.'

'Well, keep your distance, darling. Make him a colony at most. Certainly not a *département*.'

She gives a weary chuckle. 'Obviously, I shan't be going to Tuscany with them now; I'll stay with you, if that's all right. And later – well, who knows?'

And maybe the children will want to come with her to Cornwall in August, she says; they'd like to see the eclipse, and me. In any case, he can't bully her any more into keeping them away from me.

She'd better think about going to bed, she says. I say, yes, get a good night's sleep; I've read her manuscript, but we can talk about that tomorrow. Her tired tone drops away instantly: 'You've read it! What do you think?'

'I like it.'

'Really?' She's excited.

'Really.'

'It's only a first draft.'

Of course, I say, there are a few things ... That moment of change from the old to the new ... but we'll have plenty of time to talk about it.

'Yes. Excuse me a moment ...' I hear her, more faintly, speaking to someone – Jeremy, his querulous voice – scolding him for still being awake, telling him to make his peanut-butter sandwich quickly and take it up to bed. Addressing me again: 'They're upset, poor dears.'

'That's natural ... Miranda darling, that passage about creating the *Jane Eyre* manuscript – that was fiction, of course?'

She laughs. 'Oh God, yes! I based that on what your girlfriend, Judith, accused me of. Do you think I'd have written it if it was true?'

'Well, that's a relief. I was sure it wasn't. Darling, I'm sorry I didn't take you to France.'

Oh, it's such a long time ago, she says; and then she asks if it's the foghorn she can hear, and I say yes. From several miles down the coast the great foghorn at Pendeen has started to boom. How it takes her back, she murmurs. I hear her say goodnight to Jeremy, and get to sleep soon. How many nights I had to do the same to her, after one of our scenes.

I ask her why she has omitted the elderly white man, the *beki*, from Miranda's amours, and she explains that she thought three men was already at the limit of credibility, in a week. Good Lord! I exclaim, her mother once ran through an entire rock band at a festival in a couple of hours! And she responds, sharply, that she's not her mother. Then, in a softer, almost childlike voice, asks if she wandered into my room in the night. Yes, I say, she was sleepwalking.

'I thought I came in. Daddy, I don't think we should do it often, if I'm staying with you for some time.'

'Do what?'

'The dressing-up, the voice, and so on. I don't mind it, I like it, but we should keep it for special occasions, I think.'

'As we have done.'

'Yes ... Anyway, coming back to Bertrand – he put on such a lovely lunch for me, and was so generous and gentlemanly. Also' – with a chuckle – 'he's the only one likely to hear about it and possibly read it if it should ever get published! He has a huge collection of novels, English as well as French.'

'That's a good point!'

Her voice changes again as she blurts out: 'God, I'm going to have a baby!' With a little skirl of happy panic. Then, quieter, almost dreamily – 'I think I set out to get pregnant. I want this child to be just mine. And, maybe a little bit, ours ... Mum's too ... Does this make any sense? I've drunk too much wine and whisky.'

'It does make sense, darling.'

'I think so,' she says; and continues in a soft, distant voice, 'The three of us will look after him, or her.'

I swallow the lump in my throat, to reply, 'We will.'

'That's why I made the tape. I can see it now; I didn't really know why, at the time. But I wanted to involve us all.'

What tape? I'm about to say; but she yawns and says she's knackered. We exchange our goodnights. I'm only a few paces from the phone when it rings again, making me jump. I go back and pick it up. Her voice sounds lighter: 'Daddy, I'm sorry, I just wanted to say ... sometimes I've felt held back by you, by the house, the memories ... but it isn't really so. I do feel *free* there, with you, as I don't anywhere else. So it's a positive decision to come home ... Goodnight.'

'Goodnight.'

My heart dances as I pour myself a nightcap, then sit with it facing seawards. The curtains are drawn back; the house is enshrouded in blackness. How strange, I muse, that she referred to feeling 'held back'. I couldn't have been more liberal; never stopped her having boyfriends, got our GP to talk to her about contraception, encouraged her to go for university. Women are as mysterious as the black turbulent ocean out there.

I'm loath to go to bed; but at last I make the effort. On my way to the stairs, seeing an unfamiliar reddish gleam on the hall-table, I remember her little giftwrapped package. She was probably expecting me to refer to it and thank her. My memory's going. I tear off the gay paper, which she's cut, I notice, from one of Emma's old birthday rolls. A tape. Wrapped round it, a message from her. I take it back to the living-room where I've left my magnifying glass.

'*Moments intimes, Martinique. Et tu penses que je ne t'aime pas!*'

15

Maison Maréchal Ney,
Diamant,
Martinique.

March 18 1843

Dear Mrs Ashford,

Forgive this letter from one who is unknown to you. I am a freeborn Negro residing in a village in the south of Martinique. My age is three and twenty. Few Negroes of this island are free, although it cannot be many years before the same rights are granted here as have been granted on the English islands. I grew up conscious of being privileged – yet scorned by most of those who were white, and envied – detested even – by those of my own colour; those in chains, those subject to cruel punishments; those for whom the deadly *fer de lance* snake had been imported into our forests to deter attempted escapes. However, I digress. I must tell you something of my life.

I was raised in the austere household of a priest, in the village of Le Morne-Rouge, nestling under the flanks of la montagne Pelée. I was informed that my mother had abandoned me and that I owed my life and good fortune to the priest's intercession and benevolence. I had a few vague childish memories of life on a great plantation, and of being cared for, but nothing substantial that I could bring to bear against the words of the priest: indeed, how can priests lie?

It was no life of luxury, I had menial tasks to perform and scant food; but I must give *Mon père*, as I was taught to call him, credit for giving me a good education – so good, in truth, that I can define in a single word the penalty he exacted for that good education: I became his catamite, from the time when I was about eight years of age.

Two years ago I fled from his kindly care, and found work as a docks storeman in the capital, St Pierre. I had never before been to St Pierre, and was overwhelmed by its beauty. I took mass regularly at the beautiful cathedral, and became known there – as a Negro who could not only speak French well, but could read it! And who could speak English also, and even knew Latin!

It was thanks to this minor local fame, that I became drawn to the attention of a remarkable English lady, a little younger than I. I cannot and do not wish ever to forget the moment when this young lady, accompanied as I thought by a much older servant, approached me as I left the cathedral. In a shy voice, she apologised for this unorthodox *rencontre*, but believed I might be able to assist her in her quest. She introduced herself as Mrs Rochester, and her companion (not servant as I had assumed) as Madame Maillard. You are more familiar with the first lady, madame, as Jane Eyre, just as you were better known to her as Miss Temple. As for the second lady – I know that Jane wrote to you before setting sail for Martinique, and so she may have mentioned that she was being accompanied by one Grace Poole. She married a French sailor during the voyage, hence the French appellation for someone who was English in a very down-to-earth way.

You may, by now, have some inkling of where this is headed. Grace – though it was long before I referred to them so familiarly – had once had charge of a poor, mad Creole woman called Bertha Rochester, born Bertha Mason. You know that story … at least the version believed by Jane. When the three of us found shady seats near the cathedral, I was offered a startlingly original picture of my life that I could not take in; and when I began to take it in, I could not believe it.

Their story was this … (I omit details that are well-known to you, though of course they had to be explained, over and over, to me.) There was an heir to an English estate living on Martinique, they believed. Jane wished to find him. They had visited the *plantation* Mason, where they had been received coldly and unhelpfully by the present owners, but enquiries among the older slaves had pointed them to the priest at Morne-Rouge … The priest confirmed that a boy had been given into his care, given his name (DuBois), with a sum of money. *Mon père* had seen no reason to hide the truth; he was proud that he had cared for me well, and educated me to a high standard. Ungratefully I had run off … He believed, to St Pierre.

Jane's enquiries among the educated people of the capital had led to me … She showed me a drawing, supposedly of me in the arms of my white mother. You will not be surprised to know that I wept. She looked so beautiful, so kind … If only she *were* my mother! I still could not believe it, you see. So then the English lady, small and neat in her white dress and with her white parasol, showed me the statement which *Mon père* had written and signed. It was true!

Jane confessed to me, on our second or third meeting, that

it had been a considerable shock to discover that I was black. My mother had had a dusky complexion, but not so dusky as to prepare anyone to confront a Negro ... Nor did the drawing give any hint that I differed in complexion from my mother.

Yet Jane – Mrs Rochester – my stepmother! – was already, she said, becoming used to me; and could even see points of similarity in my features to those of her late husband. Only I was comely, handsome – she flattered me by saying – whereas my father had been only attractive in an ugly way!

I learned from Grace how bitterly my poor mother had grieved for me, and never forgotten me – and I wept again.

We took a boat from St Pierre to the slave-port of Diamant. I had never before been on the sea; I was fearful and very sick. It was my first time also in the south of the island. Everything was new and wondrous to me, though my heart felt sick at the sight of the slaves, the Congos, being brought ashore, half-dead from their detestable voyage below deck. Jane, so humane, proud that the English had abolished slavery, pointed out to me Le Rocher du Diamant, which she said had been occupied by English sailors during the war. She spoke it proudly. I felt, and feel, Martiniquain; it did not matter to me who owned the island, whether they were French or Spanish or English.

The coach took us to my birthplace, away up the forested mountainside. I looked at the lovely plantation house, and at the toiling slaves; but we did not stay there, returning to Diamant. The purpose of this visit was for them to call again on an old man, a former slave of the plantation, who had been freed for saving his master's life. Before, when they had called on him, Jane had not been able to understand him; yet she suspected he knew much.

We found him in his hut, gutting evil-smelling fish, which almost drove the ladies out. Skeletal and feeble, he was obviously pleased to see them again; pleased with the bag of coins placed in his hands. I was able to interpret his words. Though he had worked in the fields, he had been close to my mother's maidservant. Everything that went on was thus reported, and spread as swift as hot lava around the plantation. The mistress was so happy! She loved the Englishman so much, and he adored her, you could see ... Only, when the black child was born, it was a great shock for both of them. The master could not believe he was the father of this devil-child. She had sworn she had been faithful; and everyone who knew her best – that is to say, her household servants – knew this to be true. She wanted no one but him, she wanted no one else's *lapin* in her *patate* ... This was a colourful Creole way of describing my mother's deep fidelity to my father, and the old man's toothless mouth rounded into a laugh as he uttered it.

Anyone on the plantation could have told the master about Bertha's grandmother, who solaced herself for a cruel, drunken husband by choosing among the young Negro slaves. Her offspring were white, or white enough, but everyone knew of cases where the black blood came up again, thirty, forty years later ...

The old man was becoming agitated, speaking more quickly through his gummy lips, so that I too found him hard to follow; but I could understand that my father started to treat my mother badly; he beat her, and went off for months at a time. And so eventually, she started to pay him out by taking other lovers. And her behaviour grew more wild ... Yes, yes, she became a bit crazed ...

The master went out of his mind too when he found out

164

about her lovers, because he was still in love with her, wanted her only for himself; and the mistress could be heard sometimes laughing, goading him with her conquests. And that was when he made up his mind to take her to England, and to leave the devil-child behind. But maybe he wasn't entirely sure the child was someone else's, because it was said he left enough money for him to be well cared for and educated.

After he'd finished talking the old man grasped my hands in his and said, 'Your mama was a good woman. God bless you!'

'And God bless you!' I managed to say, though my voice was choking.

We returned to Diamant. Jane set about renting a house, overlooking the sea. She took it for a month, after which they were due to return to England – and Grace to rejoin her new husband. Jane begged me to live in the house with them. I agreed to do so. I could be useful to them; it was not easy for two Englishwomen, on their own. It was convenient for me to be regarded as their houseboy, to preserve their reputation.

I spent a good deal of my time with Grace, for I wished to draw on her knowledge of my mother. They had been closer, over many years, than are most married couples. I was glad to hear that my mother was not always insane; and that when her mind was clear she was a loveable companion.

As Grace learned to trust me, and to enjoy talking with me, she told me certain personal things which astonished and upset me. They were things which I thought Jane had a right to know about; but Grace said she had kept them back because she knew they would add greatly to Jane's distress over my father's death. Jane was a strong character, I said, and she would ultimately be helped by knowing the truth. Grace promised to think about it.

I had become attached to Jane, with whom I was spending much time. She was attempting to persuade me to come back to England with them, to claim my inheritance – while warning me that affairs were in disarray. I was determined not to go; I was and am a child of the sun, of the tropics; and I had no wish to take possession of a mansion where my mother had been made to suffer so much. Jane at last accepted my decision. She pressed a large sum of money on me – even though I knew she was not well off – and said she would do her utmost on my behalf when she arrived home.

But mostly, walking along the shore in the early morning, or late in the evening, we did not talk of business. She did much to add to my scant knowledge of England, its customs, literature and architecture. And of course we talked more personally. She confessed to great guilt that she had not regarded my mother with more pity. She spoke, with anguish, about her marriage – how it had not been consummated. This touchingly honest confession took place before Grace's revelations to me.

I write this slowly; it is already two weeks since I began it; I must check many words in the dictionary Jane gave to me. And also the memories are quite painful.

One day, a week before Jane and Grace were due to sail, I was sitting on the shore, at sunset, flicking flat stones across the water and wondering what I should do with my life. I thought of starting a school with the money Jane had given me. The great Diamond Rock glittered under the late rays. I saw Jane running barefoot towards me; as she drew near I saw she was crying. She collapsed sobbing at my feet. I reached out my hand and stroked her hair, seeking to console her –

instantly apologising for daring to touch her. For answer she took my hand gently in hers. Then she stammered out to me what Grace had just told her; and I pretended to be surprised and shocked.

I convey this confidence to you because I know she confided to you the sorrows of her marriage. According to Grace, my father had never lost his desire for, his obsession with, my mother. Every few months, usually during a drinking bout, he would visit her, and Grace would be compelled to restrain her, to an extent, while he enjoyed his marital rights. Grace had felt that, after all, they were married; she must obey him. He said he had no other outlet, *could* have none other. All of his supposed mistresses were bravado, gross exaggerations. No one can love like Bertha, he told Grace.

And then, one year, my mother was again with child. My father was aghast. Termination was out of the question for religious reasons, though Grace offered. The only solution was to let her have the child and then send it away abroad. My father found an indigent French lady – one of his supposed mistresses – who would take a child on, for considerable recompense. A surgeon named Carter was also present at the birth of a girl. She was removed at once, to become 'Adèle', a French actress's love-child. My mother, during her pregnancy and after, was mercifully lost in clouds of unreason and forgetfulness.

Grace was not sure why my father eventually sent for their daughter. She guessed the expenses were proving onerous. A governess in his own house would be cheaper.

'And that's when Jane Eyre came.' Jane herself spoke those words, wistfully to me. According to Grace, my father continued to have occasional relations with my mother, right up to her death. But he became fond of Jane Eyre; he hated his obsession, longed for a normal life. He hoped Jane would provide it. But his ideal – his passionate – image, Bertha, my mother, stood in the way.

And she could be jealous still: for my father came to her before his first 'wedding', and goaded her with his new bride. Bertha tricked Grace into letting her escape, and she tore up Jane's wedding garments. Poor woman, it was all she could do.

Perhaps wisely, Grace chose not to reveal this last detail to Jane; nor did she choose to tell her that my father sent for her several times after my mother's death: finding some comfort in her talk, even asking Grace to *impersonate* my mother to some extent, because she had known her so intimately; pretend to *be* her, leading him to a degree of arousal and satisfaction.

After his marriage to Jane, his sight improving, he rode to visit her sometimes, including on the very day of his death, seeking, through her, some shadow of his lost love.

What circumstances Jane had been told were quite distressing enough; but gradually, as the light failed on the beach, I succeeded in calming her. The news about Adèle truly shocked her; for Adèle, she said, was as white as I was black. Immediately after, she said, 'I did not mean to be offensive, Robert – I *like* your blackness!' and gave a wan smile. 'It is not a blackness of character; far from it.' And she raised herself to kiss my cheek, saying softly, 'Thank you.' My eyes met, close-up, those extraordinary, luminous eyes of hers.

I helped her to her feet, and we walked back to the house, where Grace was in turmoil wondering if she had done wrong.

She was able to offer Jane one consolation, swearing as to its truth. It helped her considerably, though it was bittersweet to me. The freed slave, she said, had wronged my father, and dealt too leniently with my mother. It was natural that slaves should prefer to protect one of their own, an islander, even their mistress, against an interloper. Bertha had told her, several times, during sensible interludes, that her husband had always treated her kindly – as he continued to do at Thornfield Hall: never beaten her, never got drunk in those early days, never left her on her own for long, never been unfaithful. *She* had strayed often, from the first, stealing out at night to meet someone. Because she simply could not stand being tied down, imprisoned, in marriage. She had been 'a bad wife', she told Grace. Far from beating her, she had sometimes struck *him*, and found him peculiarly responsive to her savagery.

'She couldn't bear feeling chained up, miss,' Grace said; 'but when she was mad, of course she had to be.'

She imparted, to me alone one evening, that he had come to want – to demand – abuse and anger from my mother, on the occasions when he visited her for his rights. She, Grace, needed to sedate her enough with gin, beforehand, to tame her madness to an extent, but not to remove her wild, angry spirit completely. It was difficult for Grace, and she drank too much herself on those occasions. I suppose my own history of being abused permitted me to listen to Grace without horror, and so encouraged her to be honest.

She recalled the last time he had ridden to her humble cottage, wild-eyed, bleeding from cuts he had suffered in his headlong ride through the woods. He had demanded punishment for having so gravely wronged Jane, and for a long time she had abused him and treated him violently, as he required. He rediscovered his manhood on these occasions – though Grace insisted they never had sexual intercourse. When he was dressed again, he shared her supper of bread and milk. Over it, he begged her to come back to Thornfield Hall, when it was rebuilt, saying that with her strongminded presence as a counterweight, he might be able to make his wife tolerably happy; indeed, she might gradually 'train' her to be more pleasing to him. But Grace had no wish to submit herself to such an existence, and refused his offer. He became very upset again, and as if careless of his life; it was dark by now, she urged him to stay the night for his own safety, but he left, in as demented a state as when he came.

I agreed with her it would serve no purpose for Jane to know these things. However, in the course of time, when Jane had grown stronger, I did little by little apprise her of all I knew.

There was one matter of immediate concern to both Jane and myself. If my mother was promiscuous, how could we be certain I was Edward Rochester's son? How could *Grace* be so certain? We asked her, and she told us. My mother had no doubts of it, she told Grace; since invariably, with other men, she had insisted on a form of intercourse which ensured the woman would not become with child. Grace described it bluntly, in her down-to-earth way. Poor Jane was disgusted and disbelieving. I assured her it was a not uncommon practice among my people. It is something I had come to know all too well, but in an exceedingly unnatural form.

Jane was consoled that my father had, after all, been a decent man; a man grossly wronged. For myself, I felt compassion for both my parents. I write this so that *one* other person, at least, may feel sympathy for them both.

The time for my ladies' departure was fast approaching. I helped them to pack their trunk, but I could not bear to wait to see them set out; even less, to see their ship disappear over the horizon. I determined to leave before them; and as there was no ship ready to sail for St Pierre I decided to take the coach to Fort Royal. The parting was very painful, on both sides. The coach was half-way to Fort Royal when I ordered the driver to stop and turn round. We reached Diamant at nightfall. They were astonished to see me. I asked Jane to walk with me on the beach. She accompanied me, wondering. 'Have you changed your mind about coming to England?' she asked.

'No, Jane.'

'Then – what?' She stopped, and we confronted one another.

I whispered, 'Will you marry me?'

Her little hand flew to her bosom, which began to heave. 'Oh! ... Oh, good heavens! I did not expect this!'

'Nor did I.'

She fought to quieten her breathing, then murmured, 'I think I love you. No, I *know* I love you. But – how can I marry you, since I was married to your father?'

'That is true.' I drew her to me and we kissed. 'But stay here, at least for a time. What have you to go back for?'

'Nothing! Nothing!'

So she stayed. She rented our little house for another two months. You would not have recognised pale Jane, for she, and Grace too, enjoyed the freedom of drawing in the sun, almost naked at times, so that they became glowing and burnished.

We saw Grace off on the first stage of the voyage to her new life, calming her anxieties and wishing her God's speed.

We lived in Diamant together; in a short time we were living together as man and wife. We did not feel any sense of sin. Through our love she was able to experience in full the

171

passion that my father could not provide for her. We both bore deep scars, but helped to heal each other; she said that our love was hard, uncuttable, like the Diamond Rock. Such was our passion, which seemed to be boundless, that we began to understand my father a little better. Hitherto, we could not at all comprehend how my poor mother's madness, and her potential violence, only served to increase his desire for her. Now Jane – and I, to a lesser extent – saw that her gentleness, her purity, had no chance of wooing him away from Bertha. She even, in the course of our passion, understood my mother a little better; understood, that is, that the heights of passion can render everything pure.

We were planning to start a school together for the local black children; and to our joy she felt stirrings in her womb.

She spoke of you often, and wished to write to you; only the consciousness that you are a clergyman's wife, and would doubtless be embarrassed and disapproving, prevented her.

I speak in the past tense because – I can hardly write it – a month ago she came down with one of the fevers of the island, and in a few days was no more. At least she did not suffer for long; and before she passed away she gave me her beautiful, gentle smile, and said she had had more happiness in our few months together than many people have in a lifetime.

I regret bitterly that we did not sail to England. She would still be alive. I regret Grace's departure, though I hope she has found happiness. She herself scarcely wanted to leave – feeling, she said, that she had made an over-hasty marriage; also that it would be painful to live so near, yet so far, from the grave of her son who drowned in childhood. I believe she became very fond of me. I have written her with the dire news, saying also that if things do not work out for her there

I would welcome her back. Our mutual knowledge of Jane would be some consolation, and the great difference in our ages would remove any possible awkwardness.

I intended to write you a short letter, but once I began it has been some relief to keep writing. Dear Jane wrote every day, in the cooler hours of the morning; and you will find her writings in the packet. She asked that I send them to you. It is her life story, begun in England after my father's death. I know that, had she lived longer, she would have presented my mother in a different, slightly softer, light. But, as she once said to me, we are all bound within the island of our time, and our upbringing, and only a great passion, a great faith, can free us from it.

Pray for her soul, and for me.

Respectfully yours,
Robert Rochester